THE TEMPLE

THE TEMPLE

A REPTILIAN ALIEN TRILOGY
BOOK 1

BY GLORIANNA ARIAS

DEDICATION

To my son JoseLuis for inspiring me to keep moving forward and survive against all odds.

CONTENTS

Preface

This story has been sixteen years in the making. Through the years, it has evolved and transformed itself in my imagination with every new experience I've encountered in life. When I first conceived of *The Temple*, I was in junior college. It was the summer of '97, and I was taking a political science class.

I originally started writing *The Temple* as a novel, though my ideas about aliens back then were quite antiquated and rather cliché, with visions of spaceships arriving from outer space and crash-landing on earth.

From the very beginning, I knew I wanted my story to be a political-thriller-slash-sci-fi-alien conspiracy, but somehow I just couldn't give it an angle that was compelling enough to make it stand out from the rest of ideas floating around in my head. Because of that, I lost interest in it and shelved it for a long time. Almost a decade, that is.

The one thing I simply couldn't get over was that the premise of my story was way too similar to the Roswell incident. It involved an alien body recovered from a wrecked spaceship.

How extraordinary is that, right? It's only the basis for a million other B movies out there.

Anyhow, the setting I'd chosen for the novel version of *The Temple* was the Strait of Bosphorus, in Turkey, and its main reveal was to be an alien/human DNA cloning conspiracy.

Even though the TV series, *The X-Files*, had already introduced this concept since the early 90s, I'd never watched it before, so I thought when I came up with something similar that my idea was brilliantly original. Boy, was I wrong!

I didn't realize this until many years after the show had ended, circa 2006, long after the first *X-Files* film had been released. I was in film school at the time and had started adapting *The Temple* to screenplay format in order to publish it as my masters thesis. For some strange reason, the story just kept coming back to me and it wouldn't leave me alone.

Given my lack of experience writing science fiction, I started doing online research about alien mythology to give my story a more convincing backdrop. This is how I discovered what later came to be known as the ancient astronaut theory, pioneered by Erich von Däniken in his 1968 book, *Chariots of the Gods?*

Aside from that, I also took a special interest in watching late night reruns of *The X-Files*, which also incorporated ancient alien ideas in its mythology. To top it all off, I spent countless hours browsing the New Age section at Barnes & Noble, reading about the so-called "reptilian agenda." This is where I became acquainted with radical books like David Icke's *Children of the Matrix*.

Still, despite all the careful research I conducted, my thesis version of *The Temple* turned out to be quite rough, with a lot of character inconsistencies and plot holes. The bottom line was that I was in a mad rush to graduate, so I did the best I could at the time and barely managed to get it approved by my thesis committee in order to pass.

I can't even begin to describe just how crushed I was by the merciless criticism of my professors during that time. They made me revise the story and heavily re-write it to the point where it felt like a house of cards that I kept having to stack up again and again after it repeatedly fell apart.

The amount of frustration I experienced during the "development-hell" phase of the story was nerve-racking to say the least. Yet, many years later, after watching the entire *Star Wars Saga* back to back and, on top of that, re-watching all nine seasons of *The X-Files* plus the two films on Netflix, I came to the realization that my professors were right in being so darn nitpicky with me.

The truth is, no matter how much it hurt, I knew their criticism was valid and, if only I were to implement their suggestions into the story, maybe I could come up with my very own epic alien mythology.

After all, in film school, I'd learned about Joseph Campbell's model of "The Hero's Journey," otherwise known as "The Hollywood Formula," so I knew I could make my story fit the model and turn it into something that would at least resemble a screenplay.

Years later, when I started watching the History Channel series, *Ancient Aliens*, my interest in re-writing *The Temple* came back with a vengeance. So much so that, at night, when I was falling asleep, I had clear visions of the movie script published as a book. Like many years before, the story simply wouldn't leave me alone. It wanted, no, more like *demanded*, to be told.

Aside from that, the one person that continued to remind me about it was my son. He'd helped me write the fight scenes while I was in college, so he knew the story quite well and he believed in it. The fact that my teenage son had faith in my story was a huge inspiration for me.

It also made me wonder about how many other teenagers might also enjoy the story if they were to see the film in theaters. This is how I came to believe that *The Temple* was a story worth telling.

That being said, the one thing I do want to make clear is that, even though it has taken me sixteen years to finish this story, I am by no means claiming it is perfect or extraordinary. First off, I must confess that, for a feature-length screenplay, it is quite long. I am well aware of it, but even then I refused to delete scenes that I consider integral to the plot and characterization.

I've heard some experts in the field say that a script must always conform to the traditional 120-page length. However, I believe that, when scenes pour out spontaneously the way they did for me while I was editing the final draft, it's a crime to go back and delete them. This is part of the reason I decided to publish the screenplay as a book. To let the full story out without constrictions of length or structure. I figured if they turn 500-plus-pages novels into movies, then how hard can it be to turn my story into a movie?

All in all, I have written *The Temple* as it came to me. I've allowed my characters to express every word they wanted to get off their chests. In my humble opinion, the resulting story has a lot more depth now than it did when I published it as my masters thesis.

If or when this script is made into a movie, I'll let the producers, editors and distributors have the last word. What is important to me now is to let the story surface as it was originally conceived, pure and unadulterated, and, above all, true to my vision.

In my perspective, *The Temple* is a far superior story now than it was when I first conceived of it. Yet, in actuality, the main thing that has changed in the past sixteen years is me.

The difference between now and then is not so much my story, but, rather, my own perspective of myself as a writer. After a long journey trying to find self-perfection in my writing, I have realized that there is no such a thing as a perfect story.

There is only what we write, and the fact that we dare to write it in the first place. The rest is all subjective. Notions of what is good and what is bad are ultimately irrelevant. What truly paves the road to success for an artist is self acceptance.

As irony will have it, there are many poorly-written books being made into movies or being labeled bestsellers in America. This goes to show that, in the end, it is the author's faith in their story that makes all the difference. I will not name any names, because that's not the point.

The point is that, after years of searching for the Holy Grail of writing, I have come to realize that writing is a process of self discovery that must be pursued at all costs. For, if one wastes precious time comparing one's stories to the legends, the masterpiece within will always fall short.

There are so many stories out there waiting to get written, so many potential authors who die with entire sagas buried in their hearts because they think they have to reach a certain level of perfection in order to be worthy of telling their story. In the meantime, it is often the mediocre writers who write and write like there's no tomorrow, caring nothing about what the critics say.

So, it is with these conclusions in mind that I'm finally letting my story face its destiny, whatever this destiny may be. I look at it like a gladiator I'm setting free in a coliseum. The arena is surrounded by an audience demanding to be entertained. The critics are beasts of prey waiting to devour it. Will my story beat the odds, or will it be deemed mediocre and disappear into oblivion like many others before it?

The only way to find out is by setting it free.

The story you are about to read is written by an author who is a lot more mature now than she was when she started writing *The Temple* sixteen years ago. Today, I have come to accept that imperfections are what make the art of storytelling such an intricate part of the human experience.

In all honesty, I have no intention of apologizing or making excuses for this story. The final version of it is as I wrote it, and I am satisfied knowing that I've done my very best in re-writing it, so I can only hope *The Temple* finds its audience. Let critics be critics, and let writers be writers. As for me, I choose to be a writer. My own worst critic at times, I admit, but a writer nonetheless.

The greatest reward I have attained throughout this journey

is one of self acceptance. I cannot ask for anything more as an author. As long as I accept my story for what it is, any other rewards that may come as a result of its publication are just the icing on the cake.

The Temple is the story that, in my heart of hearts, I wanted to tell. It goes without saying that, if I had the money to produce the film myself, I would do it in a heartbeat. But since I don't, all I can do is hope that maybe, just maybe, if I publish the screenplay as a book, a movie producer somewhere might read it and take an interest in it.

So here's hoping my dream comes true.

Act I

OVER BLACK: WE HEAR SIRENS BLARING.

TITLE: "Those conspiracies that are too incredible to be believed, are by the same right those which most often succeed."

The Dulce Book by Branton.

FADE IN:

INT. EMERGENCY ROOM - NIGHT

TITLE: UTAH, 1998.

A set of double glass doors slides open.

TWO PARAMEDICS rush in through THE AMBULANCE ENTRANCE, pushing a gurney down the hallway and toward the TRIAGE DESK.

On the gurney lies a thin and frail GIRL, 6 years old, blonde hair, steel-blue eyes. Her whole body shakes violently under the sheet. Hair disheveled, and gaze lost in the distance, she appears exhausted and disoriented.

Her lips are chapped, and there are stains of DRY BLOOD in her nostrils. She's got CUTS and BRUISES all over her body, and the slightest movement around her makes her flinch. The frightened look in her eyes indicates she's completely ON

EDGE.

INT. EXAMINATION ROOM - CONTINUOUS

The paramedics help THE TRIAGE NURSE move her to a bed, and the child projectile-vomits all over the floor.

PARAMEDIC
(handing chart to nurse)
They found her wandering naked by the side of the road.
Couldn't get a word out of her.

The nurse wipes the vomit off the child's mouth, then examines her eyes.

Her face expressionless like a zombie, the girl remains unresponsive.

While the nurse continues the examination, the paramedics exit with the gurney.

The nurse takes a closer look at the wounds and scratches on the child's limbs. She balks in shock when she notices NEEDLE MARKS.

NURSE
(thinking out loud)
Oh, God! She's been drugged.

Just then, something catches the nurse's eye. Behind the child's right ear, she discovers a DARK MARK in the shape of A SUN. She takes a closer look at it, wondering what it is.

NURSE (CONT'D)
What's your name, dear?

She's about to take her blood pressure, when the child cringes at the sight of the cuff.

NURSE (CONT'D)
(hiding cuff)
Easy, honey, it's okay. I'm not going to hurt you.
(showing empty hands)
It's gone. See?

The child relaxes, sinking back into her trance.

Gently stroking the child's hair, the nurse searches for a reaction, but the child doesn't move. The absence in her eyes is a haunting vision. It reflects an emotional detachment well beyond her years.

NURSE (CONT'D)
Can you tell me your name?

Still no response. The nurse pauses to think for a moment, then tries something else. Her tone now becomes lively, her voice high pitched, as if she were talking to a preschool child.

NURSE (CONT'D)
I guess if you don't tell me your name, I'll have to make one up for you. Hmmm, let's see.

Pretending to be deep in thought, the nurse looks at the child out of the corner of her eye.

NURSE (CONT'D)
How about a name that starts with an 'E'? Emma, Evelyn, Eve, Elizabeth, Emil—

CHILD
(interrupts)
Karen.

NURSE
Karen? That's a beautiful name.

Karen doesn't reply.

NURSE (CONT'D)
Can you tell me who did this to you, Karen?

The nurse's question appears to really hit her.

Karen tenses up, shaking with sudden terror and making tight fists with both hands.

NURSE (CONT'D)

It's okay, sweetie. You don't have to tell me about it if you don't want to.

She wraps a blanket around Karen in an attempt to comfort her.

NURSE (CONT'D)

You're safe here, honey. No one's going to hurt you anymore, I promise.

INT. NURSES' STATION - FIFTH FLOOR - NIGHT

Later that night, TWO NURSES stand behind the counter, filling out paperwork.

A LAB TECHNICIAN with a tray full of NEEDLES advances past the counter and into:

INT. KAREN'S ROOM - CONTINUOUS

The lab tech comes in and stands by the bed.

LAB TECHNICIAN

Hello there. I need to borrow your arm for a second, okay?

Karen doesn't answer, so the lab tech proceeds to tie a rubber band tightly around her upper arm.

LAB TECHNICIAN (CONT'D)
I need you to make a fist like this, alright?

He prepares the needle to draw Karen's blood.

LAB TECHNICIAN (CONT'D)
You're going to feel a little sting, but it'll go away real fast.

The second the lab tech sticks the needle into her vein, Karen SNAPS. She lets out A LOUD SCREAM and KICKS HIM IN THE STOMACH with such force that she sends him flying through the window, CRASHING through the glass and down several stories to his DEATH.

CUT TO:

EXT. HELIPAD - HOSPITAL ROOF - NIGHT

A BLACK HELICOPTER lands on the helipad, and USAF COLONEL NATHANIEL PRESTON, 40s, climbs down from it, followed by A MILITARY DOCTOR and AN ENTOURAGE OF SFs (Security Forces) armed with M-4 rifles.

INT. KAREN'S ROOM - MOMENTS LATER

In a corner behind a broken table, Karen crouches down like a hunted animal ready to attack.

Colonel Preston enters first and fixes his eyes on hers, observing her for a short moment, then assessing the WRECKAGE all around him.

He shakes the hand of the DOCTOR who waits in the room.

NATHAN
I'm Colonel Nathaniel Preston, Wing Commander at Hill Air Force Base.

DOCTOR
Would you care to explain what the hell is going on here, Colonel?

NATHAN
We're here to clean up the mess. That's all I can disclose.

DOCTOR
Oh, let me guess! Classified government information, right?

NATHAN
(to SFs)
Put her in the chopper.

DOCTOR
Wait a second! You can't just take her. She just killed one of

my lab techs.

NATHAN

If you keep her here, you and your staff will be dead by morning. Is that a risk you're prepared to take, Doctor?

Struck dumb with shock, the doctor steps aside, watching as an SF aims a TRANQUILIZER GUN at Karen. As we see the expression of dread on the doctor's face, we hear the gun GO OFF.

EXT. HILL AIR FORCE BASE - NIGHT

The black chopper arrives at the base.

INT. MAXIMUM SECURITY FACILITY - CONTINUOUS

Nathan takes Karen to a testing facility with TREADMILLS and CARDIO MACHINES, OBSTACLE COURSES, MONITORS and all sorts of ELECTRONIC DEVICES.

MONTAGE:

Karen runs on a treadmill with electrodes attached to her head and chest, while Nathan and the military doctor watch her heart rate on a monitor. They both stare at the monitor in awe.

Karen's heart rate and running speed are so abnormally fast, that the treadmill breaks down.

Karen lifts weights using various weight machines.

Nathan and the doctor can hardly believe it as she lifts 1,500 pounds with very little effort.

Karen dashes through a grueling obstacle course with great ease and precision as Nathan and the doctor time her. Neither man can believe the child's coordination and superhuman speed.

INT. LAB - NIGHT

Nathan and the doctor sit in front of a one-way glass, watching Karen, who is in A PADDED CELL.

The child HOLLERS loudly, leaping up and down the walls like a wild animal.

KAREN (O.S.)
Let me out of here. Let me out!

NATHAN
Why isn't she responding to the sedatives? She's been up for 48 hours straight.

MILITARY DOCTOR
We gave her more than four times the normal dose already.

Giving her more could kill her.

Nathan watches the screen, thinking. A few minutes later, he stands up.

NATHAN
(determined)
I'm going in there.

MILITARY DOCTOR
Colonel, please. It's not safe.

NATHAN
Watch the screen and only call for assistance if I ask you to. Is that clear?

MILITARY DOCTOR
(shaking his head)
But, Colonel—

Nathan exits.

INT. CORRIDOR - CONTINUOUS

Two SFs carrying tranquilizer guns stand outside Karen's cell as Nathan walks over to them, salutes them, and then motions for them to step aside.

He slides open a small window in the door to talk to her.

NATHAN
Karen?

INT. OBSERVATION ROOM/INT. CORRIDOR - INTER-CUT

Karen comes to the door and looks at Nathan through the window.

KAREN
(pouting)
I want to go home.

NATHAN
You're never getting out of there acting like that.

KAREN
Please let me out.

NATHAN
I need to come in and talk to you. Can I do that?

KAREN
(hesitant)
Okay.

Nathan pulls out a set of keys and unlocks the door.

INT. CELL - CONTINUOUS

He steps in, followed by the SFs. Karen stares at the tranquilizer guns, then timidly takes a step back.

NATHAN

If you behave like a normal little girl, we won't ever have to shoot you again. You understand me?

Karen nods, her eyes bouncing back and forth between Nathan and the SFs towering behind him.

NATHAN (CONT'D)
(beckoning)
Come here.

She approaches cautiously, with an air of skepticism in her eyes.

KAREN
Please let me go home.

He kneels down in front of her and smiles, trying to appear friendly, but Karen remains serious, guarded.

NATHAN
I'm afraid that's not possible, dear.

He comes closer to her, moving her hair aside to examine her mark.

KAREN
Why not?

NATHAN
(ignoring her question)
How did you get this mark? Did someone do this to you?

KAREN
No. I was born with it.

He grows uneasy. She narrows her eyes, trying to figure him out.

KAREN (CONT'D)
Why can't I go home?

NATHAN
(avoiding her eyes, staring at the mark)
This is your home now.

Karen shakes her head no repeatedly.

KAREN
(at the top of her lungs)
No! Where is Patrick?

She starts SCREAMING, exploding into a furious rage as AN INVISIBLE FORCE seizes Nathan and violently SMASHES him against the wall.

Reacting instinctively, the SFs aim the guns at her, but Nathan stops them right as they're about to pull the trigger.

NATHAN

No, wait, don't shoot, I'm alright.
(getting up, realization hitting)
She grows stronger every time we shoot her.

Karen backs away slowly, scared of her own TELEKINETIC POWERS.

For a brief moment, all three men look at each other in shock.

Noticing the frightened look on the child's face, Nathan approaches her once more, this time slower than before.

NATHAN (CONT'D)

Calm down, dear, please. Let me help you, okay? Tell me.
Who is this Patrick you speak of?

Karen's lip trembles, and she hesitates before answering.

KAREN

My little brother.

Nathan pauses to think.

NATHAN
I didn't know you had a brother. Where is he?

KAREN
He got away.

NATHAN
How?

KAREN
I helped him.

Karen's words make Nathan swallow hard, but he quickly tries to hide his concern.

NATHAN
(in a casual tone)
How, uh, how old is he?

KAREN
Four and a half.

NATHAN
He's much too young to be out there all alone, don't you think?
(shooting a suggestive glance at SFs)
He won't survive out there on his own.

(to Karen)

You wouldn't happen to know where he may have gone, now would you?

Karen notices his silent exchange with the SFs.

KAREN

No. Why are you asking me that?

NATHAN

Because he's your brother, dear. You don't want anything bad to happen to him ... right?

Pouting, Karen lowers her eyes and shakes her head no.

NATHAN (CONT'D)

I guess we'll have to find him then.

FADE OUT.

OVER BLACK: John Holt's reggae song, "POLICE IN HELI-COPTER," plays in the background as we:

FADE IN:

EXT. JUNGLE - DAY

TITLE: COLOMBIAN JUNGLE, SOUTH AMERICA. 15

YEARS LATER.

ESTABLISHING SHOTS OF:

A VAST COCA plantation. INDIGENOUS FARMERS, both male and female, work the fields.

Several GUERRILLA SOLDIERS, MEN, WOMEN and even TEENAGERS, saunter around the plantation, armed to the teeth with AK-47 rifles, walkie-talkies, hand grenades, the works.

Nearby, a DRUG LAB, also heavily guarded by GUERRILLA SOLDIERS.

Inside the lab, numerous stacks of plastic bags, full of powdered cocaine.

WORKERS ooze in and out of the lab, busy with various tasks involving the distilling and processing of COCA LEAVES.

AERIAL VIEW OF THE JUNGLE: We move in to reveal a TINY VILLAGE, a few miles from the plantation.

EXT. DIRT ROAD - CONTINUOUS

A U.S. AIR FORCE HUMVEE drives down the road and heads toward the village.

INT. HUMVEE - CONTINUOUS

KAREN, now 21, drives the humvee.

Her straight, long hair is pulled back into a pony tail. As she adjusts her sunglasses, we zoom in towards her neck and recognize the SUN BIRTHMARK behind her ear.

She wears a pair of army green shorts and a tanktop, black combat boots and a USAF ball cap.

EXT. VILLAGE - CONTINUOUS

A group of LOCAL CHILDREN play near the road as Karen drives by.

They wave at her, and she waves back.

CHILDREN
Hola Capitán.

She blows them a kiss, and they take off running after the humvee, trying to catch up with it, but the humvee soon disappears into the dense jungle beyond.

EXT. TRES ESQUINAS AIR BASE - DAY

Karen's humvee arrives at a small base that is nestled in the midst of a dense tropical foliage.

We can tell by the SOLDIERS' UNIFORMS that the base
is jointly occupied by U.S. and COLOMBIAN MILITARY
FORCES.

Karen parks the humvee and gets out, then opens the back to
take out a large wooden crate labeled "PLAN PATRIOTA."

As she struggles to carry the heavy crate inside, we see that she
NO LONGER HAS THE SUPERHUMAN STRENGTH she
had as a child.

INT. BASE - CONTINUOUS

Karen trudges in with the crate and runs into JEFF LARSON,
her CHIEF MASTER SERGEANT, Caucasian, dark hair, mous-
tache, early 30s. He seems to be in a rush and about to leave.

An unspoken tension passes between them as he quickly takes
the crate from her.

KAREN
(slightly blushing)
Hey, Chief. Leaving so soon?

Much taller than Karen, the chief is an attractive man with a
square jaw, bronze skin and a svelte, muscular physique. His

broad shoulders and narrow waist enhance his imposing figure.

CHIEF LARSON

Seems like I'm hardly here anymore, huh?

Karen shyly steals a glance at him while he places the crate on a table. As he rushes toward the exit, we catch a glimpse of long-ing in Karen's eyes. Her back to him, she bites her lower lip.

KAREN

Another meeting?

CHIEF LARSON

No, I got some business in town I gotta take care of. Will be back tonight. Any mail for me?

KAREN

No, sir.

CHIEF LARSON

Alright. I guess I'll see you later then.

Karen waves him goodbye and heads for the table where he just placed the crate.

We notice a subtle hesitation in Larson as he turns around to leave.

In his face, we see that the strictly-business attitude he projects towards Karen is merely a front. In actuality, he's more like a high school kid getting nervous around the girl he likes, but he does his best to hide it.

He's barely stepped out of the building, when he suddenly does a 180 and pokes his head back in.

CHIEF LARSON (CONT'D)

Oh, and, uh, Captain? Colonel Preston called. I forgot to leave a note on your desk. Sorry!

Karen's face brightens up with cheerful surprise.

KAREN

(walking towards her office)
Thanks, Chief.

INT. KAREN'S OFFICE - CONTINUOUS

A sign on her door reads "Captain Samuels."

As she strolls in, whistling a jolly tune, we see that the wall by her desk is plastered with NEWSPAPER CUTOUTS, SATELLITE PICTURES, COMPUTER PRINTOUTS and countless other documents, all dealing with a terrorist known as EL LIBERTADOR (the Liberator), an elusive guerrilla leader who looks like a cross between Ché Guevara and Jim Morrison.

Some of the headlines read, "El Libertador Strikes Again: Two More Air Force Base Computers Hacked," "Colombia's New High-Tech Weapon: El Libertador," "El Libertador: Latin America's Bin Laden?"

Karen turns on her computer and, while she waits for the OS to load, she picks up the phone and dials a number.

EXT. TEMPLE SQUARE - DAY

TITLE: TEMPLE SQUARE. SALT LAKE CITY, UTAH.

It's a warm July day, and HUNDREDS OF PEOPLE are gathered at the square, watching A PARADE. Hanging round a GROUP OF MILITARY OFFICERS, we see Nathan.

His cell phone rings, and the name "Karen" flashes on his caller ID.

NATHAN
(smiling)

Karen! I was hoping you'd call. How's everything down there?

EXT. TEMPLE SQUARE/INT. KAREN'S OFFICE - INTERCUT

Removing her ball cap, Karen relaxes back into her chair and rests her legs on the desk.

KAREN

Great, Dad.

NATHAN

(baffled)

Wait. Did you just call me "dad"?

KAREN

Yes, silly. I miss you. Haven't seen you in forever. You're always so busy.

NATHAN

Aww! I miss you too, sweetheart.

KAREN

Where are you, anyway? What's all that noise in the background?

NATHAN

Oh, I'm in Salt Lake City.

As Nathan talks on the phone, we realize SOMEONE IS WATCHING HIM.

MARCUS, Latin American, late 40s, dressed in a Hawaiian shirt and wearing dark sunglasses, struts around taking pictures of the temple. He pretends to be a tourist, but we can tell he's actually eavesdropping on Nathan's conversation.

KAREN
I thought you were in Turkey this week.

NATHAN
I was, but they flew me out for the Governors Parade. I have to give a speech tonight.

Loud STATIC interrupts the conversation.

NATHAN (CONT'D)
(indistinctly)
He's after me.

More STATIC.

KAREN
(worried, straining to hear)
What did you say?

NATHAN
I said I've got to give a speech.

KAREN
Yeah, but you said something else after that.

NATHAN
(distracted, waving at people)
I don't think so, dear.

KAREN

If there was something wrong ... you'd tell me, right?

NATHAN

Of course, honey. Now cheer up. Tell me how you've been.
Did the nightmares go away?

CLOSE ON: KAREN. A LOOK OF DISTRESS flashes across
her face as a HAUNTING MEMORY invades her mind.

FLASHBACK: INT. DARK ROOM - NIGHT

We catch a BRIEF GLIMPSE of AN ELDERLY WOMAN with
LONG, GRAY HAIR. Her face is extremely wrinkled, like
she's hundreds of years old. We find out she's blind because her
eyes are WHITE with NO PUPILS. She WHISPERS something
in AN UNKNOWN ANCIENT LANGUAGE, and then the
vision vanishes.

                                        BACK TO SCENE:

INT. KAREN'S OFFICE - CONTINUOUS

Karen takes her feet off the desk and presses her bent knees
against her stomach, getting into a fetal position.

Just then, her nose starts bleeding, so she quickly wipes it with a
tissue.

KAREN

Please don't mention that. I don't want to talk about it.

NATHAN

I'm so sorry, honey. I didn't mean to upset you.

Suddenly, SOMEONE taps Nathan on the shoulder and interrupts the conversation.

It's LIEUTENANT RICKMAN, one of his fellow officers from Hill Air Force Base.

LIEUTENANT RICKMAN
Colonel?

NATHAN
(to Karen)
Listen, dear, I gotta let you go. Call me later, okay?

Karen lets out a sigh of frustration and rolls her eyes like this happens all the time.

KAREN
Okay, be safe. Bye.

By the time Karen says goodbye, Nathan has already hung up.

We can tell by her facial expression that she's really frustrated.

EXT. TEMPLE SQUARE - DAY

As Nathan chit chats with the lieutenant, Marcus continues to stalk him. Hiding in the crowd, Marcus starts coming closer and closer until he is just a few feet behind Nathan.

At that point, Marcus presses A BUTTON on his camera. The moment he presses the button, the camera starts emitting AN ELECTRONIC SOUND. Nathan hears it and grimaces in pain.

LIEUTENANT RICKMAN
Colonel? Are you alright?

NATHAN
What's that noise?

LIEUTENANT RICKMAN
What noise?

Marcus hides in the crowd, always remaining close to Nathan and continuing to press the button on the camera.

Meanwhile, Nathan looks around, frantically covering his ears and trying to figure out where the noise is coming from.

His knees buckle underneath him, and he has to hold onto the lieutenant's arm in order to keep from collapsing. He grows pale, and we see that he's growing weaker by the second.

NATHAN
(grimacing in pain)
Aaah! Can't you hear it?

Confused, Lieutenant Rickman tries to listen closely.

LIEUTENANT RICKMAN
I can't hear anything.
(waits for a response)
Colonel?

Just then, Nathan's eyelids close, and he falls to the ground unconscious. Lieutenant Rickman kneels down next to him and takes his pulse.

LIEUTENANT RICKMAN (CONT'D)
(speaks into radio)
Headquarters, come in. I have an officer down. I repeat. Officer down. I need an ambulance in Temple Square right now!

CUT TO:

EXT. JUNGLE - DAY

Back in Colombia, A MILITARY CARGO TRUCK drives up A WINDING TRAIL, then stops to drop off A BLACK OPS TEAM.

Karen, their captain, jumps out first, signaling for her men to follow her.

Now wearing her CAMO UNIFORM and GEAR, Karen leads her squad deep into the jungle.

EXT. TEMPLE SQUARE - DAY

Meanwhile, in Salt Lake City, AN AMBULANCE arrives to pick up Nathan. Out of it climb TWO PARAMEDICS.

One of them is LITA, who appears to be in her early 20s.

Her hair is pulled back into a ponytail, and she has LONG RAS-TAFARIAN DREADS.

The other paramedic is A BEARDED MAN with a suspicious look on his face.

LITA
(taking Nathan's vitals)
How long has he been unconscious?

LIEUTENANT RICKMAN
At least ten minutes.

Lita helps the bearded man place an oxygen mask on Nathan's face. Then, they put him on a gurney and load him up into the ambulance. Soon after that, the ambulance takes off, SIRENS BLARING.

EXT. JUNGLE VALLEY - DAY

Back in Colombia, Karen silently assigns positions to each of her men, directing them to take cover behind the rocks and bushes.

Karen takes out her BINOCULARS and starts spying on THREE GUERRILLA SOLDIERS.

She soon discovers that they are headed for A STRAW HUT.

One of the three guerrilleros, JUANITO, mid 20s, keeps an eye out for danger and remains a few steps behind the other two guerrilleros, who continue moving forward towards the hut.

CLOSE ON: Juanito as he adjusts A SMALL ELECTRONIC DEVICE in his front pocket.

INT. MOUNTAIN CAVE/EXT. JUNGLE VALLEY - INTERCUT

Chief Larson has set up camp in the cave. Looking at his SATCOM SCREEN, he types in a few commands, and the LIVE FEED on the screen becomes clearer.

We see that the small device Juanito adjusted is really a HIDDEN CAMERA that is communicating via satellite with the chief's satcom.

This is how we find out that Juanito is actually A MOLE posing as a guerrillero.

EXT. JUNGLE VALLEY - CONTINUOUS

Once the guerrilleros have entered the hut, Karen turns to REGIS, GOMEZ and BRAVO, three of her men, who are standing by behind her. She signals for them to follow her. Then, as she leads them closer to the hut, she motions for the rest of her team to spread out and seal off the area.

Tapping on her collar, she activates her COM-LINK TRANS-MITTER.

KAREN

Alright, Chief, target location is secured. Awaiting clearance to proceed.

Karen waits for a response and, as soon as she hears it, she talks to her men.

KAREN (CONT'D)

Clearance granted. Let's go!

Careful not to make a sound, Karen and her three men advance slowly towards the hut.

As they get closer, she gives a thumbs up to A SNIPER who hides in a treetop above them.

EXT. MOUNTAINTOP - CONTINUOUS

A GUERRILLA WATCHMAN looks down at the valley below through a PAIR OF BINOCULARS.

It appears he's been watching EVERYTHING.

INT. HUT - CONTINUOUS

Karen kicks the door down and aims her M-16 rifle at the guer-rilleros who just went inside.

KAREN
Freeze.
(yelling in broken Spanish)
¡Nadie se mueva, manos arriba!

EXT. MOUNTAINTOP - CONTINUOUS

The guerrilla watchman talks Spanish into A RADIO and noti-fies the person on the other end that they've got problems.

WATCHMAN

Soto a Base, repito, Soto a Base, tenemos problemas, cambio.

INT. HUT - CONTINUOUS

The guerrilleros eyeball each other as they put their hands up in the air. The looks of confusion on their faces make it obvious they've been caught off guard.

Karen's men follow her into the shack and point their M-16s at the people inside.

A LITTLE BOY, around 5, who sits on a cot in the back corner of the hut, starts crying as soon as he sees the rifles. Standing by a small propane stove, A WOMAN takes a step forward towards the boy, but Karen warns her not to move.

KAREN
(to woman, in broken Spanish)
Deténgase, señora.
(into com-link)
Chief, we got a mother and a child in here.

INT. MOUNTAIN CAVE - CONTINUOUS

Chief Larson's eyes are glued to his satcom screen. He sees the woman and the child in the hut.

CHIEF LARSON

Keep them safe, and proceed with the mission.

INT. HUT - CONTINUOUS

The boy screams louder, so Karen beckons to him, trying to get him to come to her, but the boy refuses to move. His LOUD SCREAMS add to the tension already filling the hut.

KAREN

(into com-link)

Copy that, sir.

With her finger firm on the trigger, Karen takes a deep breath in an effort to keep it together.

She keeps aiming her M-16 cautiously at the guerrilleros while she takes the boy's hand and leads him toward his mother.

The boy quiets down as soon as he's in his mom's arms.

Babra positions herself in front of the mother and the boy to protect them. She then nods and gestures for her men to go to the guerrilleros.

KAREN (CONT'D)

Relieve them of their weapons.

As her men move towards the center of the hut and force the guerrilleros to lie down flat on the ground, Karen suddenly HEARS NATHAN'S VOICE ECHOING IN HER HEAD.

NATHAN (O.S.)
Karen! Help me!

Careful not to lose sight of the guerrilleros in front of her, Karen looks around disoriented.

KAREN
(deeply worried, whispering to herself)
Nathan.

Just then, A FLEETING VISION INVADES HER MIND. She sees Nathan chained to a metal chair, his head slumped in front of him as though he were passed out.

Karen's nose starts bleeding again.

BRAVO
Captain? Is everything okay?

Without letting go of her rifle, Karen quickly rubs her nose against her shoulder to wipe off the blood. She makes an effort to concentrate on her teammate's words, but she can only hear INDISTINCT ECHOES. Her vision has temporarily consumed her attention.

CUT TO:

EXT. TEMPLE SQUARE - DAY

Back in Salt Lake City, the festivities continue as Lieutenant Rickman paces anxiously back and forth, talking on his cell phone.

LIEUTENANT RICKMAN
What do you mean they're not at the hospital yet? They left here over an hour ago!
(shakes his head in frustration)
Preston. Colonel Nathaniel Preston. How many times do I have to tell y—

All of a sudden, the ground beneath Officer Rickman's feet starts VIBRATING. Thrown off by it, the officer ends the call abruptly and places his cell phone in his pocket. He stands still and quietly notices that the vibration is gradually crescendoing. Before he knows it, the vibration has turned into AN EARTH-QUAKE.

Glancing over at the people around him, he realizes they are reacting to it, too. He watches in shock as the crowd slowly begins dispersing.

LIEUTENANT RICKMAN (CONT'D)
What the—

Soon, the earthquake becomes more and more intense until A THUNDEROUS, RUMBLING SOUND emerges from below the ground and RESONATES OMINOUSLY throughout the square.

PEOPLE SCREAM and panic, scurrying desperately in all directions. Everyone is disoriented, not knowing where to go.

Just then, the streets around the temple CRACK OPEN, and that's when Officer Rickman realizes this is NO ORDINARY EARTHQUAKE. He discovers that the ROARING SOUND is coming from THE TEMPLE, so he sprints away from it, trying to alert the crowd as he goes.

> **LIEUTENANT RICKMAN (CONT'D)**
> Get away from the temple!

Everyone retreats fast, following the lieutenant's lead.

The moment he reaches a safe distance away from the square, Rickman can't help but stop and turn around. He stares in awe as the temple suddenly EXPLODES into A HUGE BALL OF FLAMES.

EXT. TEMPLE SPIRES - CONTINUOUS

E.S. Posthumus' remix of Bach's "ST. MATTHEW PASSION" plays in the background as we see the GOLDEN STATUE of

ANGEL MORONI flying through the air in slow motion, then crumbling into a thousand pieces as it crashes on the ground.

EXT. STREET - CONTINUOUS

A MASSIVE CLOUD of flames and flying debris swallows up Temple Square. People scatter about, wounded and bleeding, screaming hysterically, and trying to get away from the fire.

Cars explode and crash into each other while the traffic lights go berserk.

Lieutenant Rickman reaches for his radio as he watches in horror. What started out as a happy celebration has quickly turned into UTTER CHAOS.

CUT TO:

INT. HUT - DAY

Back in the jungle, Karen has barely recovered from her strange vision, but she still appears pale and distressed.

She continues to stand in front of the woman and her child as Bravo and Gomez, her teammates, search the two guerrilleros.

With a murderous glint in their eyes, the guerrilleros lie belly down on the ground, staring directly at Karen with their arms tied up behind them. We can tell by the way they look at her that they've figured out she's the one in charge.

Meanwhile, Juanito, the mole, and Regis, Karen's other team-mate, look through some papers that are stacked on a small wooden table against the back wall of the hut.

REGIS
Captain, I think I just found something you're gonna want to see.

KAREN
Thanks, Regis. Keep an eye on the family for me, will you?

Regis nods and trades places with Karen.

Appearing a bit more calm, Karen heads over to the table to join Juanito. On top of a mess of papers and computer printouts, she finds A SET OF BUILDING SKETCHES and BLUEPRINTS.

KAREN
Looks like some kind of underground building. See the surface here? Superficie, ¿comprendes?

CLOSE ON: Sketches and blueprints. We follow Karen's fingertip as it slides across the sketch of AN UNDERGROUND BUILDING.

The building is shaped like a mushroom, with a large dome on the top and supported by a multilevel cylindrical structure that appears to reach hundreds of feet into the ground.

JUANITO
(with a heavy Spanish accent)
Sí, I heard them talking about thees, capitán.

KAREN
What about this other building here? ¿Qué es ésto?

She points at the sketch of yet another building drawn on the surface above the underground dome, A GOTHIC-LIKE STRUCTURE with TALL SPIRES and BATTLEMENTS.

The surface and underground buildings are connected to each other by A NETWORK OF TUNNELS.

JUANITO
I don't know, capitán. I only heard them talk about it one time and that was it.

Karen puzzles over the sketch.

KAREN
I think it's some kind of palace. Hmm... how do you say? ¿Palacio? I wonder if it's something they plan on bombing.

JUANITO

I don't think so.

Karen examines Juanito's expression and notices he's intimidated by the guerrilleros lying on the ground, but she still insists.

KAREN

What do you think it is, then?

JUANITO

(shrugging his shoulders)

¿Tal vez una catedral?

REGIS

A cathedral?

Karen nods affirmatively as she continues to stare at the sketch.

EXT. TREETOP - CONTINUOUS

Outside the hut, Karen's sniper suddenly spots SEVERAL GUERRILLEROS emerging out of the jungle.

Forming a circle around the perimeter of the hut, the guerrilleros close in fast.

SNIPER

Oh shit!

INT. HUT - CONTINUOUS

Meanwhile, Karen continues analyzing the blueprints as Juanito digs out A PRINTOUT from the stack of papers on the table.

KAREN
Let me see that. Hmm . . . Looks like he was comparing prices for airplane tickets.

JUANITO
Sonora, Mexico.

KAREN
Maybe that's where the cathedral is.

The moment Karen says this, one of the guerrilleros on the ground yells a threat in Spanish at Juanito.

GUERRILLERO
¡Te vas a arrepentir, hijo de puta!

Bravo presses the rifle hard against the guerrillero's back.

BRAVO
Cállate la boca.

KAREN
What did he say?

JUANITO
He says I'm gonna regret this.

Karen rolls up the blueprints and sketches, and sticks them in her backpack.

KAREN
We better get out of—

Before she can finish her sentence, the sudden sound of SHOTS BEING FIRED outside interrupts her.

REGIS
(looking through window)
Everyone down. We're surrounded!

Karen quickly dives toward the woman and child and drags them down to the ground. The child starts SCREAMING AT THE TOP OF HIS LUNGS.

KAREN
Shh ... silencio, hijo.

As Juanito and the other teammates drop down for cover, Karen gets on the com-link.

KAREN (CONT'D)
Chief, our position's been compromised. Target location's under

enemy fire. We need a rescue helo dispatched right away. Do you read me?

EXT. TREETOP - CONTINUOUS

The sniper aims his rifle at the hordes of guerrilleros closing in on the hut from every direction.

He empties several rounds in an attempt to keep the guerrilleros from advancing any further, but he can hardly keep up. There are way too many of them, not to mention they are expert chameleons and know just how to blend in effortlessly with the jungle brush.

EXT. BUSHES AROUND HUT - CONTINUOUS

The rest of Karen's strike team has been standing by outside the hut. The moment they see the sniper has opened fire on the guerrilleros, they come out of their hideouts and confront them head on.

INT. CAVE - CONTINUOUS

Meanwhile, the chief gets on the com-link with Karen.

CHIEF LARSON

Okay, captain, rescue helo's on the way. What's your position?

INT. HUT/INT. CAVE - INTERCUT

Karen lies face down on the ground, covering the boy and his mother while scrambling to find a way out. The child BAWLS desperately as the bullets zoom closely past them.

> **KAREN**
> We're trapped in the hut, sir. I can't move.

> **CHIEF LARSON**
> Get your men out of there as soon as you can and keep moving, understood?

> **KAREN**
> Yes, sir. How much longer until helo arrives?

> **CHIEF LARSON**
> Five minutes at the most. Keep your eyes open.

Just then, A HAND GRENADE lands on the hut's roof, instantly blowing it off the top.

Karen presses her hands down on the heads of the mother and the child to keep them from looking up.

EXT. TREETOP - CONTINUOUS

Watching the roof burst into flames distracts Karen's sniper temporarily, and he pays dearly for it. He almost loses his arm as he takes a hit on the shoulder.

He is about to fall off the tree, when he quickly grabs a hold of a branch just in time to avoid a disastrous death.

Without hesitation, he immediately resumes his attack on the guerrilleros, shooting down a few of them. But his victory is short lived, for he soon takes another hit, this time on the leg. Yet, even then, he bravely keeps shooting.

EXT. BUSHES AROUND HUT - CONTINUOUS

The teammates sealing off the area continue exchanging fire with the guerrilleros, doing their best to keep them from getting through to the hut, but many of them are growing weaker, as they've taken hits and are now wounded and bleeding.

MORRIS, one of the teammates who's been shot in the chest, can no longer hold up his rifle to shoot, so he crawls behind a tree stump instead and gets on the com-link to warn Karen.

MORRIS
(tapping collar)
Captain, you need to get out of that hut now. We're losing ground fast. I repeat. We are losing ground. We won't be able to hold them back for much long—

Before he can finish talking, a bullet penetrates his head and kills him instantly.

INT. HUT - CONTINUOUS

Karen slams her fist on the ground in despair and frustration as she hears Morris' death live through the com-link.

But her own situation is far too critical as it is, so she doesn't even have time to say a prayer for her fallen comrade. She's too busy struggling to avoid being hit by the burning pieces of roof that are raining down on her.

To make matters worse, right at that moment, one of the straw walls catches fire, and A DENSE CLOUD OF BLACK SMOKE rapidly spreads out inside what's left of the hut.

The child and the mother start COUGHING, and, soon after that, Karen and her teammates follow suit.

In a last-ditch effort to survive, Karen rolls toward the back wall of the hut and uses the butt of her M-16 to poke a hole through the straw.

KAREN
Everyone out, let's go!

She pushes the boy out through the hole first. Next, she helps the mother out. After that, she evacuates her teammates.

By then, the two guerrilleros on the ground have passed out from asphyxiation, so Karen manages to pull them out just seconds before the hut's walls begin to collapse.

EXT. BURNING HUT - CONTINUOUS

Once they've all made it out safely, Karen and her teammates quickly take cover behind a ROCK FORMATION a few yards behind the hut. The mother and the child remain hiding behind Karen, while the two guerrilleros are still passed out on the ground.

Just then, another HAND GRENADE lands on the hut, resulting in a BLAST that barely misses Karen's group and forces them out of their hideout.

That's when one of the guerrilleros surrounding the area spots them and immediately warns his fellow fighters.

Karen opens fire on the approaching guerrilleros, making sure that the mother and the child are behind her at all times.

KAREN
(to teammates)
Fire at will!

Karen's teammates follow her orders and start shooting at the guerrilleros.

EXT. TREETOP - CONTINUOUS

In the mean time, the sniper is still at it, shooting down guerrilleros left and right, now focusing on the ones closing in on Karen's group. He hollers with joy when he sees THE RESCUE CHOPPER finally appearing in the sky.

EXT. CHOPPER - CONTINUOUS

The PJs (PARARESCUE MEN) aboard the helo shoot down at the guerrilleros, clearing the way for Karen's group.

EXT. ROCKS BEHIND HUT - CONTINUOUS

Having spotted the chopper, Karen springs up from the ground and grabs the woman and the child by the hand.

KAREN
(to child)
¿Estás bien, hijo?
(to woman)
¿Señora?

They both nod affirmatively, still dumbfounded.

KAREN (CONT'D)
Bravo and Regis, each of you escort one prisoner to the helo.
I'll interrogate them later.

Bravo and Regis grab a hold of the guerrilleros, who are so weak
and faint from having inhaled all the smoke, that they have very
little strength to resist.

KAREN
Juanito, I'm putting you in charge of protecting the civilians.
Gomez and I will clear the path for you.

JUANITO
Entendido, Capitán.

Juanito picks up the child and takes the hand of the woman, but,
just as he's about to head for the chopper, AN ANGRY MOB OF
GUERRILLEROS ambushes him.

ANGRY GUERRILLERO
¡Traidor!

KAREN
(to Gomez)
Buy me some time, will you?

GOMEZ
I'm almost out of ammo, Captain.

KAREN
I just need a couple seconds.

Gomez gets in front of Juanito and starts shooting at the angry mob, while Karen ducks down, opens her backpack and takes out A GRENADE LAUNCHER.

By then, the angry mob has gotten too dangerously close to Gomez, and his ammo is all out. Luckily, Karen manages to fire a grenade just in time to push back the mob and, once the path is cleared up, she leads her group straight towards the:

INT. CHOPPER - CONTINUOUS

Regis and Bravo are already on board with the prisoners by the time Karen's group arrives there, so they help them climb inside, while the rest of Karen's strike team remains on the field, holding off the guerrilleros that are trying to come after the chopper.

KAREN
(into com-link)
Chief, we need reinforcements to evacuate the rest of the team. Morris is down, and there might be more casualties.

CHIEF LARSON (O.S.)
(into com-link)
Let *me* worry about the evac, captain. You just get home safely, understood?

The chopper takes off as Karen and her teammates cheer and high five each other.

The only unhappy people there are the two prisoners.

The woman and her child smile at Karen with gratitude. Karen smiles back at them, satisfied. She checks her backpack to make sure the blueprints and sketches are still in there.

HARVEY, the pilot, African American, mid 20s, smiles as Karen sits next to him.

KAREN
Thanks, Harvey. Let's go home. I think we
got what we came for.

FADE TO:

INT. BASEMENT - TRES ESQUINAS BASE - NIGHT

Later that night, Chief Larson sits at a desk. The lights are dim, and he's all alone in the basement. He appears relaxed in his camo pants and tank top. Staring at his laptop screen, he reviews the VIDEO FOOTAGE he captured from Karen's mission in the jungle.

Just then, he hears A NOISE, so he gets up and heads toward the door to investigate.

Right as he opens the door, he runs into Karen who is just walking in. As he towers over her, she shies away, intimidated by the sheer size of him.

CHIEF LARSON
(smiling, flirting unintentionally)
Jeez, Captain, what are you doing up so late?

Karen's hair is still wet from the shower she just took, and she's out of her combat uniform. The jean shorts, flip flops and tanktop she's wearing go well with her petite figure, and Larson cannot help but notice it.

KAREN
Sorry, sir. I didn't realize you were here.

CHIEF LARSON
Why aren't you in bed? Didn't you get my message? I gave you a day off. Take advantage of my generosity.

KAREN
I couldn't sleep.

CHIEF LARSON
I see. Well, why don't you go grab a beer or something?

KAREN
Maybe some other time. I'm here to interrogate the prisoners

we captured today.

CHIEF LARSON

That's *my* job, Captain. Now, if you don't mind, I've had a rough day and I'd like to chill for a bit. You should do the same.

KAREN

Forgive me, sir, but no. I don't want to chill. Not while those men are sitting on sensitive information we could be using right now.

The chief is taken aback by Karen's bold attitude, but he quickly brushes it off and doesn't make a big deal about it.

CHIEF LARSON

Well, you're off duty right now, so do me a favor and bring it up during our meeting the day after tomorrow, comprende?

He goes back to the desk, sits down and goes back to reviewing the footage on his laptop. Unwilling to give up, Karen sits across from him and stares directly into his eyes to get his attention. He casually glances over at her, holding back a smile.

CHIEF LARSON (CONT'D)
What?

KAREN

I really need to find out what those men are up to, Chief.

CHIEF LARSON

You fulfilled your part of the mission successfully. Now go on home and get some rest. I got this.

KAREN

I don't mean to question you, sir, but Nathan sent us to retrieve those documents for a reason.

CHIEF LARSON

Of course, and we will get him the intel he wants in less than 72 hours like he asked. Why the sudden rush?

Karen gets up from the chair and starts pacing nervously in front of his desk.

Shaking his head in disapproval, Larson pauses the video he's watching and gives her his full attention. Karen is suddenly flushed, unable to resist the weight of his stare, so she averts her eyes and quickly turns her back on him to keep him from noticing she's blushing.

CHIEF LARSON (CONT'D)

Captain, listen to me. You got nothing to worry about. I'm sure the Colonel will be very proud of you when he finds out what you accomplished.

KAREN

Something happened today, sir. And I'm really worried about

him.

CHIEF LARSON
He's got an entire security detail attending to his every need.
What can possibly happen to him?

KAREN
Have you heard from him since this morning?

CHIEF LARSON
No.
(pauses to think)
Well, to be honest, I haven't had a chance to check my messages
yet, but—

Without letting him finish, Karen rushes toward the fax machine
by his desk and starts going through the stack of incoming faxes.

CHIEF LARSON (CONT'D)
What are you doing?

KAREN
Checking your faxes, sir. Look. Three days worth of important
messages.

CHIEF LARSON
What is it you expect to find?

KAREN

Nothing. I mean, I hope he's okay, but I have to be sure. I've been trying to call him since I got back, and his cell phone keeps going straight to voicemail.

CHIEF LARSON

In case you forgot, Captain, the Colonel is a busy man.

KAREN

I just talked to him this morning, and he was in Salt Lake City. He had to give a speech for the Governors Parade.

CHIEF LARSON

Oh wait. Temple Square, right?

KAREN

Yes!

CHIEF LARSON

Okay, now that you mention it, my secretary did say something earlier about a Lieutenant Rickman trying to reach you from Temple Square.

KAREN

And why didn't you tell me?

CHIEF LARSON

I was planning on telling you at our meeting.

KAREN
(panicking)
Did he leave a callback number?

CHIEF LARSON
I would assume he did. I left the note upstairs in my office.

Without saying a word, Karen spins around on her heels and takes off running toward the elevator. Larson follows after her.

CHIEF LARSON
Wait. Where are you going?

KAREN
(getting in the elevator)
To your office.

He rushes to catch up with her and barely manages to squeeze in through the elevator doors before they slide shut.

CUT TO:

CLOSE-UP SHOT OF A COMPUTER SCREEN: A YOU-TUBE VIDEO uploaded by a civilian who captured THE TEMPLE EXPLOSION on his smart phone camera.

WIDER TO REVEAL:

INT. LARSON'S OFFICE - NIGHT

Later that night, Karen's eyes are glued to Larson's computer screen. As the camera pulls back slowly, we realize she's the one watching the YouTube video.

CLOSE ON: Karen's face. Her expression zombified from the shock, she stares blankly at the screen.

Meanwhile, Larson appears nervous and agitated, not knowing what to do with himself. He opens a file cabinet and pulls out a small bottle of Colombian whiskey he's got hidden all the way in the back behind some hanging folders. He takes a long swig straight out of the bottle.

We see the wheels spinning in Karen's head as the video comes to an abrupt end.

As soon as Larson realizes the video is over, he approaches his desk carefully and lowers the volume on the speakers. Clearly, he's being really cautious so as not to push Karen over the edge.

She appears really tense.

LARSON
(sheepishly)
Whiskey?

Karen glances over at the bottle, her mind elsewhere.

KAREN
Nathan's alive.

Larson scratches his head, trying to think of something to say.

KAREN (CONT'D)
He wasn't there when it happened, right? Isn't that what Lieutenant Rickman said in the message?

CHIEF LARSON
Captain, I know this may be difficult for you to accept, but the truth of the matter is that ... the colonel is missing.

He puts his hand on her shoulder in an attempt to comfort her.

CHIEF LARSON (CONT'D)
The ambulance that took him vanished without a trace.

Karen collapses into Larson's chair.

KAREN
I knew he was in trouble. I *knew* it.

CHIEF LARSON
But how? Did he say something to you?

KAREN

No, not exactly, but, this morning, when I talked to him on the phone, I thought I heard him say, "He's after me."

CHIEF LARSON

(narrowing his eyes)

Who?

Karen thinks for a moment, then something suddenly dawns on her.

CHIEF LARSON (CONT'D)

What is it?

She does an image search on Google and finds a picture of the Mormon temple, then shows it to him.

KAREN

See the spires on the temple?

CHIEF LARSON

(examining the picture)

Yes. Why?

Karen springs up from the chair and storms out of the office.

Moments later, she comes back with the sketches she found in the hut and lays them flat on top of Larson's desk.

KAREN

We recovered these from the Libertador's hut today. They're
printouts from the Pentagon's computer system, sir.

CHIEF LARSON

Okay, so he's a hacker. We were expecting to find that.

Karen points at the building with the spires.

KAREN

Yes, but don't you see a resemblance?

She points at the temple's picture on Larson's computer, then
back at the blueprints. Raising an eyebrow, Larson appears
confused.

CHIEF LARSON

There are countless buildings with spires all over the U.S., not to
mention Europe—

KAREN

But what if it was all planned? What if "he's after me" means
that the Libertador is actually after Nathan? The-hunter-
becomes-the-hunted kind of thing?

CHIEF LARSON

It was a *girl* driving the ambulance, Captain. A girl with dreads.
And a bearded man. It's in the lieutenant's report.

KAREN

Of course. The Libertador wasn't going to be stupid enough to show up there himself. He would've been identified on the spot.

CHIEF LARSON

Listen, I don't want to play devil's advocate here, but don't you think you're stretching the facts a little too much?

KAREN

Nathan knew he was up to something. That's why he sent us to retrieve the blueprints. We were too late.

CHIEF LARSON

Wait, but didn't Juanito tell you the Libertador is in Mexico?

KAREN

Sonora.

She finds SONORA on a map and shows it to him.

KAREN (CONT'D)

Notice how close Sonora is to the U.S.-Mexican border? Think about it, Chief. How else does a celebrity terrorist enter the U.S. undetected?

CHIEF LARSON

Okay, fine. Let's say you're right. Let's say the Libertador crossed the border illegally and that he is, in fact, behind all this.

Why come after the Colonel?

KAREN

Because Nathan is in charge of all the counter-terrorism opera-
tions in Latin America, and the Libertador probably figured it
out.

Larson shakes his head in disagreement.

CHIEF LARSON

And how would he know the Colonel was going to be there. At
that specific temple, exactly at that time?

Karen paces around, searching for an answer.

KAREN

He's a hacker, Chief. The best one we've ever dealt with. And
besides, he might have an informant, an insider. I don't know.

CHIEF LARSON

Can I tell you what I really think, Captain? I think you're over
exhausted and you need to take a couple days off—

KAREN

Why are you patronizing me, sir?

CHIEF LARSON

I'm not pat—

Turning her back on him without letting him finish, Karen takes the blueprints and places them on the SCANNER.

CHIEF LARSON (CONT'D)
What are you doing now?

She flicks him a defiant look.

KAREN
I'm officially requesting your permission to go to Utah, sir.

CHIEF LARSON
Please tell me you're kidding.

KAREN
Absolutely not.

CHIEF LARSON
I hate to sound pesimistic, Captain, but has it occurred to you that maybe the Colonel is ...

He hesitates and holds back.

KAREN
Dead?

CHIEF LARSON
Yes.

KAREN

No, sir, I'm sorry to contradict you, but he's alive.

CHIEF LARSON

How can you be so sure?

KAREN

I don't know. Something tells me he's alive. I can't explain it.
Either way, I'm going there to find him. Dead or alive. I don't
care. I'm not going to stop until I find out where he is.

CHIEF LARSON

Even if it means you're dishonorably discharged from the Air
Force?

KAREN

You can get me authorized.

CHIEF LARSON

How can you ask that of me when you know I can't?

Karen refuses to back down.

KAREN

He's the only family I've got. Tell me you wouldn't do the same
if you were in my shoes.

He lowers his head and doesn't answer.

KAREN (CONT'D)
Sir?

He sighs with resignation.

CHIEF LARSON
You're asking for trouble, Captain.

KAREN
I'll take my chances.

She finishes scanning the blueprints, then transfers the files to a flashdrive.

INT. BARRACKS - DAY

Before sunrise, Karen storms in, carrying a large backpack. She rushes past the rows of bunk beds lined up against the walls.

Harvey, the pilot, is fast asleep in one of the beds. Karen shakes him until he wakes up.

KAREN
Harvey? Wake up, please. I need you to fly me back to the States. I'm going to Utah.

FADE OUT.

Act II

FADE IN:

EXT. TEMPLE - DAY

Karen and Harvey arrive in Salt Lake City by helicopter.

INT. HELICOPTER - CONTINUOUS

As Harvey lands on Temple Square, Karen gets a view from above and observes that the blast has destroyed more than half the temple, leaving in its place a HUGE, V-SHAPED CRATER with a seemingly bottomless PIT at its core.

She hangs her head in frustration as she notices that the area is now an IMPENETRABLE FORTRESS, crawling with MPs and G.I.s from every military branch imaginable.

EXT. TEMPLE RUINS - CONTINUOUS

Complete with ELECTRIFIED METAL FENCES, BARBED WIRE and YELLOW BARRICADE TAPE all around its perimeter, the disaster zone resembles a CONCENTRATION CAMP.

Aside from the MILITARY TRUCKS patrolling it, we see numerous UNMARKED BLACK VANS, CAMOUFLAGE HUMVEES, POLICE CARS, FIRETRUCKS and TACTICAL ARMORED VEHICLES, all parked in a tight line around the chain-link fences.

The moment Karen climbs out of the helicopter, THREE MPs swarm toward her, signaling for her to stop.

MP
Ma'am, what do you think you're doing? You're trespassing.

Karen shows them her USAF badge.

KAREN
I'm Captain Karen Samuels, Special Forces. I need to speak to the officer in charge please.

The MP examines her badge with skepticism.

MP
(into walkie-talkie)
General Peters, do you copy?

GENERAL PETERS (O.S.)
Come in, officer.

MP
I have a Captain Samuels here from Air Force Special Forces asking to see you, sir.

GENERAL PETERS (O.S.)
(with a cowboy accent)
Never heard of him. He ain't on my list.

MP
It's actually a *she*, sir.

He lets out a condescending chuckle as he eyeballs his fellow MPs.

GENERAL PETERS (CONT'D)
What in the hell?

Losing her patience, Karen snatches the walkie-talkie away from the MP.

MP
Excuse me, ma'am!

As they play tug-of-war with the walkie-talkie, Karen manages to speak into it.

KAREN
General, I have sensitive information about the missing colonel. It's crucial that I speak t—

Before she can finish, the MP snatches the walkie-talkie back.

MP
Give me that.
(into walkie-talkie)
Sir?

GENERAL PETERS
I know nothing about no colonel. Get her outta here.

Disregarding his reply, Karen marches forward, passing the
MPs.

KAREN
Fine. Arrest me, then.

The MPs bolt toward her, pointing their M-4 rifles in her direction. Then one of them catches up with her and restrains her,
while the other puts handcuffs on her.

Karen tries to resist to no avail as the third MP shoves her down
on the ground.

Meanwhile, having witnessed everything from the chopper,
Harvey climbs out, but is forced to stop dead in his tracks as one
of the MPs spins around and points his weapon at him.

HARVEY
(calling out to her)
Captain?

KAREN
I'm fine, Harvey, just call the Chief and let him know please.

The MPs drag her away towards A GROUP OF MILITARY

TENTS set up within the FENCED AREA.

HARVEY
Dammit.

Unsure of what to do, Harvey hesitates, taking a step towards his captain, then retreating.

Finally, a look of determination appears on his face. He hops back into the chopper and takes off.

INT. TENT - GROUND ZERO - DAY

Later that day, Karen sits on a stool, her back propped up against a metal pole in the middle of the tent, and hands cuffed behind her.

She struggles to free herself, but the cuffs are way too tight.

GENERAL PETERS, fiftyish, swaggers in, clipboard in hand, legs curved inwards like someone who rides horses all the time, and a cigar dangling from his mouth.

GENERAL PETERS
Well, well, well. Tough little lady with a smart mouth, I see.

KAREN
Are you the general?

GENERAL PETERS
Yes, ma'am.

KAREN
What am I being charged with?

GENERAL PETERS
Actually, I just heard from your chief master sergeant. Fella by the name of Larson. You got a lot of balls showing up here uninvited, missy.

Karen waits for him to continue, but he doesn't. He just stares her up and down, shaking his head no and sneering at her with an air of chauvinistic superiority.

KAREN
(ignoring him)
So ... did the chief fax you my clearance?

GENERAL PETERS
'Fraid that ain't gonna make no difference to me, ma'am.

He places the clipboard on a table and takes a puff from his cigar, while adjusting his underwear. He doesn't seem to mind Karen's disgusted look.

KAREN
On what grounds?

GENERAL PETERS

I just found me some interesting information about this Colonel
Preston of yours.

KAREN

What kind of information?

GENERAL PETERS

First, lemme assure ya. I ain't got a problem with females in the
military ...
(blows smoke in her face)
So long as they don't meddle in the men's business.

KAREN

Nathan got Congress approval for me. I enlisted as an honorary
man. Everything was done officially—

GENERAL PETERS

I know, I know. I heard the story. But I'm the kind of man who
believes women ain't allowed in special forces for a reason.

Karen tries to play it cool as she thinks on her toes.

KAREN

I'm not going to try to change your opinion, sir, but—

GENERAL PETERS

Then don't, dawg-gammit! Who in God's name's gon raise our

children if women die in combat?

KAREN
With all due respect, sir—

GENERAL PETERS
(taking off her handcuffs)
Excuse me, ma'am, but you got some nerve questioning me.
(cutting the ropes around her feet)
Now you be a good girl and get the hell outta my town before I
lose my cool.

He drags her out of the tent.

EXT. TENT - CONTINUOUS

He is about to force her into a humvee, when Karen says something that finally catches his attention.

KAREN
What if I told you I got some leads on who's behind the bombing?

Squinting his eyes, he looks at her, considering what she has just
said.

GENERAL PETERS
Alright. You got five minutes to tell me what you know.

EXT. GROUND ZERO - NIGHT

At nightfall, the general escorts Karen to ground zero, which is teeming with FIREMEN, COPS, PARAMEDICS and RESCUE TEAMS.

Some of them push gurneys loaded with WOUNDED SURVIVORS, while others haul along CORPSES in black body bags.

Bright lights illuminate the rubble and rising clouds of dust, and pieces of broken asphalt lie scattered all over the square. It's a devastating sight.

DOCTOR RAMZI KHAN, a thirtysomething American of Palestinian descent, kneels down at the bottom of the crater, near the deep pit Karen saw earlier, collecting soil samples into small plastic bags.

GENERAL PETERS
Watch your step, Captain. Doctor Khan?

The doctor turns around and gets up when he sees the general approaching. Brushing the dirt off his pants, he notices Karen struggling a bit to walk in the rubble as she follows behind the general.

The doctor stares her down, twisting his lips in quiet disdain.

DR. KHAN
(bobbing head slightly)
General.

GENERAL PETERS
I'd like to introduce you to this here young lady. Name's Captain Samuels, Black Ops South America.

Dr. Kahn removes one of his latex gloves to shake Karen's hand.

DR. KHAN
South America. How exciting! I take it your work down there
must involve the guerrillas.

KAREN
That's right.

DR. KHAN
Interesting.

GENERAL PETERS
Dr. Kahn is Chief Investigator in the case. He's a geologist specializing in underground explosions. Ain't that right, Doctor?

The doctor nods with a glint of pride in his eyes.

Taken aback, Karen looks at the general, then back at the doctor.

KAREN

Did you say underground?

DR. KHAN

(reading her expression)

Yes.

Karen sinks into deep thought.

GENERAL PETERS

Listen, why don't I leave you two to get better acquainted? The
captain here's got some interesting theories to share with you,
Doctor.

Karen squats down by the pit, trying to find its bottom, but it's
too dark for her to see.

KAREN

Thanks, General.

GENERAL PETERS

Well ... y'all know where to find me. So long.

He climbs out of the crater.

KAREN

(to doctor, pointing at the pit)

Is that where the blast came from?

DR. KHAN
(nodding)
Correct. It shot up vertically from below the ground.

Karen rises back up to her feet, gazing in awe at the unfathomable pit below her.

DR. KHAN (CONT'D)
We're still trying to determine the exact distance.

That's when Karen suddenly remembers something.

KAREN
Do you have a computer here, Doctor? There's something I'd
like to show you.

INT. TRAILER - NIGHT

Dr. Khan and his TEAM OF SPECIALISTS have set up a
MOBILE SCIENTIFIC LAB inside a large RV parked near
ground zero.

Equipped with SEVERAL LAPTOPS, MICROSCOPES,
METAL DETECTORS, A SEISMOGRAPH, and various other
measurement devices, the RV boasts the latest state-of-the-art
geotechnology.

As the specialists climb in and out of the RV, studying debris and soil samples, Karen hooks up her flashdrive and prints out copies of THE BLUEPRINTS and SKETCHES she scanned in Colombia. She shows them to the doctor.

KAREN
My strike team seized these sketches in Colombia yesterday. They were appropriated by a terrorist known as "El Libertador." You may have read about him in the news. He's working in con-junction with the communist guerrillas in the South American jungle.

DR. KHAN
I'm not sure I follow.

KAREN
I have reason to believe these blueprints are an illustration of a facility built subterraneously under this temple. It can be accessed through these tunnels. Look.

DR. KHAN
An underground facility, huh? And with tunnels, no less. I wonder what the Mormons would have to say about that.

With a dismissive chuckle, he examines the printouts.

KAREN
It's quite possible if you consider the fact that Utah is located above a massive cavern system.

His lips twist into a condescending smile.

DR. KHAN

So you're suggesting the explosion came from the underground facility? Provided there's such a thing to begin with.

KAREN

Either that or somewhere in the tunnels, yes.

DR. KHAN

Let me just make sure I'm understanding correctly. You're not suggesting this explosion was caused intentionally, are you?

KAREN

Yes, that's exactly what I'm saying.

DR. KHAN

You mean as in a terrorist attack?

KAREN

Why not? It's reasonable to suspect a terrorist attack under the circumstances.

He stares at her dumbfounded as if she's just said the most preposterous thing in the world.

DR. KHAN

It's hard to swallow to say the least, but I can see how some-

one in your position would come up with uh ... shall we say, an
extravagant theory like that.

KAREN
What's so extravagant about it? It makes perfect sense.

DR. KHAN
Believe me, Captain, I understand it must be tough to pursue
terrorists down in the jungle day in and day out. It takes its toll
after a while I'm sure.

He eyes her with indifference as he pours himself a cup of
coffee.

DR. KHAN (CONT'D)
Coffee?

Karen folds the printouts and puts them in her pocket with a
frustrated expression in her face.

KAREN
No, thanks. Last thing I need right now is another sleepless
night.

He flicks her a sideway glance.

DR. KHAN
Don't get me wrong, Captain. Calling this incident a terrorist

attack is truly tempting.

He leisurely takes a sip of his coffee.

DR. KHAN (CONT'D)
It would make a lot of warmongers in Washington happy. I'd be
sent home with a fat paycheck after doing a press conference at
the White House. Next thing you know I'm on CNN, talking to
Larry King. It would earn me my fifteen minutes, that's for sure.

KAREN
Yes. And?

DR. KHAN
It's a nice fantasy, but the truth of the matter is, it'd be inconsis-
tent with our findings so far.

Karen holds his gaze, ready for the challenge.

KAREN
What findings?

DR. KHAN
Come with me.

INT. MICROSCOPE COUNTER - CONTINUOUS

He heads toward a group of microscopes lined up on a counter, then flips on the light switch on one of them.

DR. KHAN (CONT'D)
These are samples my analysts have been collecting.

He steps aside so she can look through the lens tube.

KAREN
What am I looking for?

DR. KHAN
You see the crystal particles? They're a pink tone.

KAREN
Okay, I see them.

She glowers at him, eyebrows knitted, and waits for his explanation.

DR. KHAN
(matter-of-factly)
Behold the culprit.

KAREN
A crystal?

DR. KHAN
Sorry to disappoint you, Captain.

KAREN

(in a mocking tone)

An explosive crystal.

DR. KHAN

And a very rare one, I might add. None of the ones known to science resemble it.

KAREN

So you're suggesting the explosion was a natural phenomenon?

DR. KHAN

That's correct. It's known as a lithospheric explosion. You may have heard of it.

KAREN

Wait just one second. And you call my theory extravagant?

He smiles unaffected and takes his time to finish the coffee.

DR. KHAN

You know, Captain, the tricky thing about having larger-than-life aspirations is that they often exceed one's talents.

She swallows hard, her lips trembling.

KAREN

I'm going to prove you wrong, Doctor.

DR. KHAN
(raising an eyebrow)
And how exactly do you intend to do that?

KAREN
I'm going down there myself to find out what happened.

DR. KHAN
I hope you don't mean—

KAREN
(finishes his sentence)
The pit.

DR. KHAN
That's out of the question!

KAREN
Why is that?

DR. KHAN
Only authorized personnel are allowed down there.

She laughs, then gets serious again.

KAREN
I can get security clearance from the Air Force, plus I'll sign a waiver holding you harmless.

DR. KHAN
I said no.

KAREN
(reading him)
There's something you're not telling me, Doctor. And I'm not leaving here until you spit it out.

The doctor hesitates, debating with himself, then finally hits her with it.

DR. KHAN
Two of my specialists went down there with a ranger team yesterday.
(he looks down with regret)
They never made it back.

KAREN
All the more reason for me to go down there then.

DR. KHAN
If you insist, but you'll have to find a different way to do it, because I'm not giving you my authorization. Now, if you'll excuse me, I have to get back to work.

EXT. JUNKYARD - DAY

The next morning, Karen rides a dirt bike down a country road.

After parking in front of a fenced junkyard, she gets off the bike.

A GRUMPY-LOOKING OLD FELLOW sits in a rocking chair behind the main gate, smoking a tobacco pipe and reading a newspaper.

A DOBERMAN sleeps on the ground next to him, chained to the chair.

The fellow gives Karen a dirty look as she approaches the gate.

KAREN
Good morning, sir, are you the caretaker?

The Doberman wakes up and starts SNARLING at Karen, but she ignores it, keeping a safe distance away from the gate.

OLD FELLOW
(through gritted teeth)
Who's askin'?

She shows him her Special Forces badge, but he barely even glances at it.

KAREN
I'm Captain Samuels, Air Force Special Ops. I talked to Detective Lennox this morning, and he told me there's an ambulance that was brought here last night—

OLD FELLOW

This is Sheriff's Department property. Only deputies are authorized to look at the vehicles.

KAREN

But Detective Lennox told me I could see the ambulance. He's
the one who gave me this address. You're welcome to call him
to verify what I'm saying.

OLD FELLOW

He's gonna have to come down here himself if he wants me to
let you in. I ain't trying to get fired if you know what I mean.

Sensing its owner's snappy tone, the Doberman rises up, this
time GROWLING at Karen even more menacingly than before.

KAREN

He's not available till the end of the week, and this case I'm
investigating is time sensitive. I can really use your help, sir.

He emphatically shakes his head no.

OLD FELLOW

'Fraid I can't do nothin' for you, ma'am.

Frustrated, Karen looks away in the distance and spots A
GROUP OF TEENAGERS riding their mountain bikes around
a:

EXT. DESERTED FIELD - CONTINUOUS

Karen gets back on her bike and approaches the teenagers.

KAREN
Hey, kids! Want to make some money?

EXT. GATE - DAY

Moments later, the kids ride their bikes towards the junkyard and start taunting the dog, bouncing up and down dirt slopes and riding around in circles in front of the gate.

The Doberman starts GROWLING and BARKING viciously at them, pulling hard on the chain and nearly knocking over the rocking chair with the old fellow still sitting in it.

OLD FELLOW
Hey!

The kids laugh and continue to tease the dog.

Furious, the old man unchains the dog, puts a leash on it and opens the gate.

He marches toward the kids, leaving the gate slightly open behind him.

As he yells at them indistinctly, and the dog goes mad with rage, KAREN shoots out from behind a tree and quickly sneaks into the junkyard through the gate.

EXT. JUNKYARD - CONTINUOUS

She sprints down countless aisles of wrecked cars until she finally spots THE AMBULANCE where we last saw Nathan.

Wasting no time, she pulls out A CROWBAR from her backpack and uses it to pry open the back doors of the ambulance. As soon as the doors open, she climbs in.

INT. AMBULANCE - CONTINUOUS

Putting down the crowbar, she takes out a pair of latex gloves, puts them on and starts digging around for possible clues.

After thoroughly searching every nook and cranny inside, she finds NO EVIDENCE whatsoever.

Everything in the ambulance has been left intact, and there appears to be nothing out of the ordinary.

Frustrated, Karen climbs out and shuts the doors behind her but, just as she's about to leave, she realizes she's forgotten THE CROWBAR INSIDE.

> **KAREN**
> (to herself, through gritted teeth)
> You gotta be shitting me.

EXT. JUNKYARD - CONTINUOUS

She now proceeds to examine the exterior of the ambulance and notices SOME SCRATCHES on the paint in the back.

Next, she squats down to look under it and notices DRY MUD on the tires. That's when something catches her eye.

She reaches behind the tire and pulls out A DRY WILD BRANCH that was caught in the axle.

As she examines the branch, she gets back up, takes out her smart phone and launches the browser, only to find out there is no WiFi.

> **KAREN (CONT'D)**
> Shit.

Careful not to make any noise, she treads swiftly down the aisle where the ambulance is parked and looks around for a way out that doesn't involve having to confront the old fellow and his dog.

Meanwhile, she takes a picture of the branch and then calls a number from her missed calls log. Someone picks up.

KAREN (CONT'D)
Chief, it's me.

INT. CHIEF LARSON'S OFFICE/EXT. JUNKYARD - INTERCUT

Pleasantly surprised, the chief springs up from his chair.

CHIEF LARSON
Captain? Where the hell are you?

KAREN
I don't have much time to talk, sir. I got no WiFi on my phone.
Can you do an online search for me?

CHIEF LARSON
Wait a second! You don't call me in two days and now you just
call out of the blue to have me do an online search? Can you at
least tell me what's going on?

KAREN
I found the ambulance where they took Nathan, sir. Looks like
it's been off-roading up in the mountains somewhere.

CHIEF LARSON
I mean, what do you think you're doing out there? I'm getting

calls here left and right. You're pissing people off, Captain.

KAREN

Please, sir, I'm in a tight spot right now. I need to find a match for a wild branch I found stuck behind the tire. Can I text you a picture of it so you can look it up for me? I promise I'll call you later to give you the full breakdown.

CHIEF LARSON
(reluctantly)
Fine, go ahead and send it.

Karen texts him the picture of the branch she just took.

Sighing with frustration, Larson enters the picture into a database and waits for the results. A map of Utah pops up on the screen.

KAREN
(getting impatient)
Any matches yet?

CHIEF LARSON
Yes, closest location is the Wasatch Mountains, about 20 miles southeast from Salt Lake City.

KAREN
Can you find out if there are any mines or cave entrances in that

area?

CHIEF LARSON
(scoffing)
Please tell me you're not still looking for those tunnels.

Karen gets distracted as she quickly scopes out the junkyard for possible exits, so she doesn't answer.

CHIEF LARSON (CONT'D)
Well, are you?

KAREN
Listen, Chief, I gotta get out of here ASAP. I could really use your support right about now.

CHIEF LARSON
Okay! Hang on.

As she waits for him to get her some answers, she hears A NOISE behind a pile of crushed cars. She freezes up, staring at her empty hand, then back at the ambulance.

A realization suddenly hits her.

KAREN
(to herself)
Shit! The crowbar.

CHIEF LARSON
What?

Just then, out from behind the pile of cars, barges THE DOBER-
MAN, now LET LOOSE FROM THE LEASH. The moment he
spots Karen, he crouches backwards slightly, GROWLING low
and mean, ready to attack.

KAREN
Oh, hell no!

CHIEF LARSON
Captain?

As the dog lurches at her, Karen spins around and hauls ass back
towards the ambulance, accidentally dropping her phone on the
ground.

CHIEF LARSON (CONT'D)
(concerned)
Captain, are you alright?

By now, Karen is long gone and unable to retrieve her cell
phone.

Right as the dog is about to pounce on her, she reaches the
ambulance. Wasting no time, she opens the back doors and
dives in.

INT. AMBULANCE - CONTINUOUS

As she tries to close the doors, the dog manages to stick its head between them, so she tries to keep him trapped there while, at the same time, she reaches behind her for A HOSPITAL GOWN.

The animal YELPS in agony, while Karen grabs the gown and ties it around the door handles to keep them from opening. This buys her a short time to turn around and retrieve the crowbar.

Meanwhile, the Doberman uses its front paws to try and squeeze through the narrow opening but doesn't get very far.

EXT. JUNKYARD - CONTINUOUS

Having heard the dog WHIMPERING, the old fellow runs clumsily toward the ambulance with A SHOTGUN in hand.

OLD FELLOW
Let him go, you crazy bitch!

He fires a shot at the back window of the ambulance, and the GLASS SHATTERS.

INT. AMBULANCE - CONTINUOUS

Barely dodging the bullet and now covered in glass shards, Karen yells at the old fellow.

KAREN
Shoot me again, and it's off with his head, you hear me?

She presses the crowbar horizontally into the dog's mouth to keep him from biting her, then unties the gown and kicks the doors open.

EXT. JUNKYARD - CONTINUOUS

The momentum sends the Doberman flying backwards in the old fellow's direction, so he immediately drops the shotgun to catch him.

Meanwhile, Karen leaps out of the ambulance and makes a dash for THE CHAIN LINK FENCE, crowbar in hand. She barely has enough time to climb up and over the fence, when the old fellow starts shooting at her.

EXT. DESERT - CONTINUOUS

Rolling on the ground, Karen manages to avoid the bullets until she's beyond their reach. Then, she sprints toward her dirt bike, which she'd left hidden in the deserted field nearby.

She jumps on the bike and takes off, leaving a crest of dust behind her.

FADE TO:

EXT. TRES ESQUINAS AIR BASE - COLOMBIA - DAY

A SMALL AIRPLANE lands on the runway.

A PETITE REDHEAD, shoulder-length hair, curvy figure, early 30s, steps down from the plane, carrying a suitcase. She wears a pair of black sunglasses and a black business suit with a white blouse showing a hint of cleavage.

We can tell by the imperious vibes she gives off, and her expensive-looking stilettos, that she is high maintenace and tightly wound. She marches toward the:

INT. SECURITY BOOTH - CONTINUOUS

Inside is A COLOMBIAN SECURITY OFFICER who is sitting back at his desk, reading a newspaper with his legs propped up on the table. When the brunette enters, he doesn't even look at her.

In an attempt to get his attention, the redhead takes off her jacket and slams it on his desk along with her suitcase. She takes out a tissue and wipes the beads of sweat off her face. The humid tropical heat is evidently a great inconvenience for her.

REDHEAD
(holding up her badge)
Agent Danielle Harris, CIA. I'm here to see Chief Larson.

SECURITY OFFICER
(chewing gum, stone-faced)
Is he expecting you?

AGENT HARRIS
No, he's not, but I need to talk to him immediately.

SECURITY OFFICER
He's not here at the moment. You'll have to wait.

With shaky fingers, the agent opens her purse and takes out a pack of cigarettes. She puts a cigarette in her mouth and lights it up.

SECURITY OFFICER (CONT'D)
No smoking allowed in here. Put it out please.

She appears so tense, it looks like she's about to snap, but, instead, she holds it in, drops her cigarette on the floor and crushes it by twisting the sole of her shoe on top of it. As soon as she's done, she flashes the officer a fake smile.

Keeping a straight face, he goes back to reading his newspaper.

AGENT HARRIS
(clearing her throat to get his attention yet again)
Officer, I just flew in all the way from Virginia and I'm exhausted. I don't have time to wait. Please get a car ready for

me. I'll go find the Chief, wherever he is.

INT. BAR - DAY

That afternoon, Larson sits at a bar, drinking rum on the rocks. He's alone and appears deeply worried, his mind somewhere else. Occasionally, his eyes flit back and forth between his cell phone and his watch.

Just then, we hear the CLICK OF HIGH HEELS approach him from behind, but he's too drunk to notice.

CLOSE ON: A WELL-MANICURED FEMALE HAND with nails polished blood-red. She offers him a cigarette.

FEMALE VOICE (O.S.)
Care for a cigarette?

Larson is so immersed in his thoughts, that he answers in a dismissive tone, without even making eye contact with her.

LARSON
No, thanks, I don't smoke.

WIDER TO REVEAL:

The hand belongs to Agent Harris, who has just walked into the bar. A little irritated by Larson's indifference, she whispers seductively in his ear.

AGENT HARRIS
Did you quit?

Larson looks at her out of the corner of his eye and, the moment he sees who it is, he does a double take.

LARSON
(surprised)
Danni?

AGENT HARRIS
Long time, no see.

She hugs him.

LARSON
What the hell are you doing in Colombia?

His speech is noticeably slurred, so she flashes him a devilish smile.

AGENT HARRIS
I just arrived less than an hour ago.

LARSON
You're here to see *me*?

AGENT HARRIS
I'm afraid so.

LARSON
Uh, oh. Should I be worried?

AGENT HARRIS
Hey, relax, Jeff. I'm just here to see how you're doing, that's all.

LARSON
(laughing, not buying it)
Yeah, sure.

He turns away from her and motions for the bartender to refill his glass.

AGENT HARRIS
Aren't you going to offer me a drink?

LARSON
I have a sneaking suspicion you didn't come all this way just to
have a drink with me.

AGENT HARRIS
Oh, come on, Jeff, give me some credit please. I've missed you
a lot. And I'm not just saying that.

He doesn't answer, so she slowly moves closer to him.

He forces his eyes open and shakes his head quickly from side to side to sober up. Then, he pulls away from her.

LARSON
(chuckling awkwardly)
You haven't changed a bit, have you?

He flicks his cell phone a furtive glance and checks his watch again.

Pretending she didn't see him do that, she waits for him to get distracted and, as soon as he looks away, she quickly turns the volume on his phone all the way down.

AGENT HARRIS
Why don't we get out of here? It's your day off, isn't it?

LARSON
Not really, no.
(cheking his watch again)
Actually, I gotta get back to the base in just a few minutes.

She grows impatient, tapping her long nails on the bar, and talks to him in a more serious tone.

AGENT HARRIS
I do have something I need to talk to you about. It's important.

LARSON
Okay, shoot.

AGENT HARRIS
No, not here. It's too ...
(looks around, biting her lower lip)
... crowded.

Reading between the lines, he stares at her for a moment, the wheels turning in his head.

LARSON
Alright, let's go to my place then.

He takes out a wad of dollar bills and slams it on the bar, then gets up to leave. Agent Harris follows behind him, a satisfied look on her face.

CUT TO:

EXT. ROAD - UTAH - DAY

Karen zooms past, riding her bike full throttle. She's got MARKS and SCRATCHES all over her body from the glass shards that fell on her in the ambulance.

As she spots a diner down the road, she slows down.

INT. LIVING ROOM - LARSON'S APARTMENT - DAY

As soon as Larson and Harris are inside, she gets rough with him and pushes him down on the sofa.

INT. ROADSIDE DINER - DAY

Karen walks in and heads toward a pay phone that is in the back by the restrooms.

INT. LIVING ROOM - LARSON'S APARTMENT - DAY

Agent Harris kisses on Larson. He appears slightly conflicted but is too drunk to resist.

INT. ROADSIDE DINER - DAY

Karen dials a number and waits for someone to pick up, but there is no answer.

KAREN
Come on, Chief, where are you? Pick up please!

INT. LIVING ROOM - LARSON'S APARTMENT - DAY

Harris starts undoing Larson's belt, when he suddenly sits up and pushes her aside, accidentally making her fall off the couch.

He makes a run for the:

INT. BATHROOM - CONTINUOUS

Larson gets sick and pukes all over his toilet. Clearly, he had way too much to drink at the bar.

INT. LIVING ROOM - CONTINUOUS

Harris is furious as she hears the LOUD RETCHING SOUNDS coming from the bathroom. With steam practically blowing out of her ears, she gets up from the floor and puts her blouse back on.

Suddenly, her eyes are drawn to Larson's cell phone, which he dropped as he got up to go to the bathroom. She bends over to pick it up, her lower lip trembling with vengeful rage, and notices he has TWO MISSED CALLS from an UNIDENTI-FIED NUMBER.

INT. ROADSIDE DINER - DAY

Karen checks her watch anxiously. She picks up the phone and dials Larson's number again.

INT. LIVING ROOM - LARSON'S APARTMENT - DAY

Harris swallows hard as she sees the call coming in. She

answers but doesn't say anything, only listens.

KAREN (O.S.)
Chief? Hello? ... Are you there? ... Chief?

Harris hangs up, a glint of jealousy in her eyes. She's so consumed by rage, that she doesn't see Larson coming out of the bathroom. He comes over quietly and stands behind her, looking over her shoulder.

CLOSE ON: Larson's cell phone. Not knowing she's being watched, Harris erases the record of the incoming calls from Larson's call log.

LARSON
(livid)
What the fuck do you think you're doing?

Harris spins around, her entire body trembling.

HARRIS
I-it was ... the wrong number.

He grabs his phone away from her.

LARSON
Give me that.

He checks his call log but there's no record of any missed calls. He then notices the volume has been turned all the way down.

His eyes bore into hers, and she takes a step back as if he were about to hit her.

HARRIS
I didn't want us to get interrupted. Babe, I'm sorry, I—

LARSON
(pointing towards the front door)
Get out.

He's calm but clearly furious.

HARRIS
Jeff, don't do this. We have a lot to talk about.

LARSON
Out, now.

Harris just stands there in disbelief as another call comes in.

This time Larson sees it and answers right away.

LARSON (CONT'D)
Hello?

INT. ROADSIDE DINER - DAY

As soon as she hears the chief's voice, Karen smiles from ear to ear.

KAREN
Chief! Oh, thank God!

INT. LIVING ROOM - LARSON'S APARTMENT - DAY

Since Harris is still standing there, refusing to go, Larson grabs his car keys and leaves the apartment without so much as putting his shirt back on.

EXT. DRIVEWAY - LARSON'S APARTMENT - CONTINUOUS

Larson rushes toward his car, still talking on the phone.

LARSON
Captain, where are you? You had me worried sick!

INT. LIVING ROOM - LARSON'S APARTMENT - CONTINUOUS

Harris walks over to look through the window and watches as Larson gets in his car and drives away, ignoring her completely. We can tell Harris will make him pay for this somehow.

INT. LARSON'S CAR - DAY

Moments later, Larson's car is parked in an alley.

LARSON
(on the phone with Karen)
You sure you're going to be okay out there by yourself?

KAREN (O.S.)
I'm fine, sir, seriously. Sorry I got off the phone so abruptly, but
I ran into a minor setback.

LARSON
It didn't sound minor. What happened?

KAREN (O.S.)
I lost my phone, but it's nothing to worry about. I'll keep you
posted. Might be a little hard to call you once I get up to the
mountains, though.

LARSON
Wait, so ... how will I get a hold of you then?

KAREN (O.S.)
I'll find a way to let you know where I'm at.

LARSON
Is there anything I can do from here?

KAREN (O.S.)

Actually, yes, there is, sir. Did you happen to find out anything about those caverns?

EXT. LITTLE COTTONWOOD CANYON - DAY

As the conversation continues in voiceover, we see Karen slowly riding her dirt bike up the canyon, using a pair of binoculars to see the cliffs in the distance.

LARSON (V.O.)

Look for the granite cliffs, up by Little Cottonwood Canyon.

She slows down to a stop as she notices a group of GIANT HALFDOME PORTALS carved out of the mountainside. Each portal is secured by BLACK IRON BARS.

LARSON (V.O.) (CONT'D)

There's a vault with access tunnels there that's owned by the Mormon Church. It's off limits to the public, though.

Karen approaches the portals, but, just as she gets close, a series of KEEP-AWAY SIGNS stop her from going any further.

One of the signs reads: "Granite Mountain Records Vault."

KAREN

Bingo!

EXT. CLUSTER OF TREES - CONTINUOUS

Hiding behind the trees a few yards from the road, we see A PUNKER/RASTA CHICK wearing camo pants, combat boots, and dog tags around her neck.

We recognize her as Lita, THE GIRL WITH THE DREADS who picked up Nathan in the ambulance.

She spies on Karen as the latter gets off her bike.

EXT. VAULT - CONTINUOUS

Karen approaches the portals and looks through the bars on a couple of them, but the place appears to be deserted.

> **KAREN**
> Hello? Anyone there?

No response. She walks over to the next portal and taps on the bars with her keys.

> **KAREN (CONT'D)**
> Hello?

Still nothing.

She snoops around some more, trying to think of what to do

while examining the area closely.

Just then, out of nowhere, coming directly from above, A HIGH-PITCHED SOUND pierces her ears.

Covering her ears, Karen looks up and freezes in shock and amazement as she catches a fleeting glimpse of A SILVER SAUCER flying across the sky at an astronomical speed.

Her nose suddenly starts BLEEDING, and she instinctively wipes it off with her hand. Deeply confused, she looks at her bloodied fingers, then back up at the sky.

> **KAREN (CONT'D)**
> (to herself)
> What the—

Wasting no time, she quickly climbs onto a tall pile of rocks and cranes her neck in an attempt to see where the saucer is headed.

She barely has enough time to look through her binoculars, when she watches the saucer disappear into A CREVICE on the side of A MOUNTAIN about a quarter of a mile ahead. Moving cautiously toward the crevice, she rubs her eyes in disbelief.

EXT. CREVICE - CONTINUOUS

Without stopping to think, Karen pulls out A FLARE from her

backpack and sticks her head through the crevice to see where it leads.

INT. CREVICE - CONTINUOUS

Looking down, she sees that it leads to A MAN-MADE VERTI-CAL SHAFT with NO BOTTOM IN SIGHT.

She's suddenly stricken by vertigo so she clutches tightly onto a rock as the cavern around her seems to spin around in circles.

She takes slow, deep breaths in an attempt to get over the dizziness. As soon as she regains her composure, she drops the flare down the shaft, hoping to get a view of the bottom. Much to her chagrin, the flare only vanishes into the dark emptiness below. She shakes her head in frustration as she pulls her head out of the:

EXT. CREVICE - CONTINUOUS

Wiping the sweat off her face and neck with a tissue, she proceeds to take out another flare, only this time she ties A STRING around it before lighting it. She then sticks her head back into the:

INT. CREVICE - CONTINUOUS

Slowly, she lowers the flare with the string and lets it slide down about 20 feet, then stops it as she catches a glimpse of A METAL LADDER attached to the shaft wall.

Sighing with resignation, Karen ties the string to a piece of broken metal that juts out of the shaft wall under the crevice.

EXT. CREVICE - CONTINUOUS

Throwing on a HELMET and CLIMBING HARNESS that she had in her backpack, Karen drills a hole in the rock and sets up her gear to descend into the:

INT. SHAFT - CONTINUOUS

She climbs down the ladder carefully, carrying a lit flare between her teeth.

She hasn't gone down ten steps, when THE SAUCER suddenly appears at the bottom of the shaft, then shoots upward in less than a second.

Stopping sharply in midair, the saucer hovers just a few feet away from Karen, producing A STRONG WIND that rocks her violently, nearly causing her to lose her grip on the ladder.

Shortly thereafter, the saucer SPEWS OUT a GOOEY WEB from its underbelly. The web is made of A STICKY, GELATIN-LIKE SUBSTANCE that attaches itself to Karen's body, and, no matter how much she struggles, she is unable to free herself from it.

KAREN
(screaming)
Let me go!

The saucer sends down A HOOK, which latches onto the web and pulls Karen up.

By then, she is so overcome with dizziness and exhaustion, that she passes out right as she gets pulled up into the:

INT. SAUCER - DAY

Some time later, Karen wakes up and finds herself lying on A FLAT, RUBBERY FLOOR.

GLOWING BRIGHT LIGHTS flood her eyes as she opens them, blinding her momentarily and forcing her to squint in order to see better.

KAREN'S POV: The vessel looks small and cozy, like the cabin of a yacht.

Shaped like a dome, its TOPSIDE HULL rises low above the floor. Its curved walls are covered with all sorts of CONTROL PANELS, CONSOLES, MONITORS and EXPOSED ELEC-

TRONIC CIRCUITS.

At the center of the saucer, she notices the BRIDGE, which is built around a CYLINDRICAL COLUMN that extends from floor to ceiling.

Karen feels a strange, itchy sensation on her skin. As she starts scratching, she finds dried bits and pieces of some clear plastic material stuck to her skin. She soon realizes it's the residue of the gooey web that caught her out in the shaft.

Noticing she still has her backpack, she checks its contents. Everything seems to be intact. She's about to get up when A HEAD suddenly pops up in front of her face.

LITA
Feeling better, Captain?

As her eyes adjust to the brightness, Karen finds herself face to face with Lita, the girl with the dreads.

Lita now wears a jacket with A SMALL INSIGNIA on the upper right chest area. The insignia is A BLACK SUN that looks exactly like the BIRTHMARK behind Karen's ear.

Karen recognizes the symbol and stares at it in amazement. Then, without thinking, she lunges forward and tries to strangle Lita.

Punches fly in every direction as both girls slam each other against the floor and walls of the strange vessel.

Much to her dismay, Karen soon learns the hard way that she's at a SERIOUS DISADVANTAGE.

Lita seems to be trained in a BIZARRE FORM of MARTIAL ARTS involving IMPOSSIBLY ACROBATIC MOVES and POWERFUL TELEKINETIC blows.

She is much too strong and fast, easily overpowering Karen on every turn. Her powers are reminiscent of those Karen possessed as a child, only Lita's moves are far more COORDINATED and CONTROLLED.

LITA
You're not ready to take me on yet, Captain.

Her lip bleeding, Karen crawls on all fours, trying to recover from the blows.

KAREN
Keep dreaming.

Karen grabs A METAL PIPE from a counter and is about to smash it on Lita's head, when Lita snatches the pipe away from her and swings it down, tripping Karen instead.

Karen stumbles down backwards, smashing her head against the floor for the umpteenth time.

LITA
I don't wanna hurt you, Captain.
(hands up in the air)
If you stop, I stop. Alright?

Lita holds out her hand, trying to help Karen up, but this only infuriates Karen more, so she grabs Lita's hand and violently pulls her down.

KAREN
You almost killed me!

As Karen tries to slam Lita's head against the wall, Lita dives head first into a front flip, spins around in midair and lands smoothly on her feet.

LITA
Kill you? I saved your life. A thank you would be nice.

KAREN
Right.

Karen scrambles to her feet and is about to spear Lita, when Lita moves aside, and Karen ends up running right smack into the opposite wall.

LITA

Captain, get a grip. You're only hurting yourself. Don't you see? In this condition, you don't stand a chance against me.

Karen pivots around into a defensive stance and stares at Lita in amazement.

KAREN
(breathing hard)
What... are you?

LITA
I'm a warrior, just like you. The name's Lita. Here.
(offers her a bottle of water)
It's store sealed, see? No tricks.

KAREN
No, thanks. I'll pass.

LITA
Suit yourself, Captain, but you're severely dehydrated. You can really use it.

KAREN
I take it you know everything about me.

LITA
You could say that.

Lita turns a few knobs on a control panel, and the column at the center rises up to reveal the STRANGEST COMPUTER SYSTEM Karen has ever seen.

It has A SPHERE-SHAPED SCREEN that looks like AN EYE-BALL. It rotates 360 degrees on its axis, allowing a three-dimensional view of the area outside the saucer.

LITA (CONT'D)
(pointing at one of the seats)
You might want to buckle up.

Karen doesn't listen. Instead, she continues to stare dumb-founded at the bizarre computer.

KAREN
What kind of computer is that?

LITA
It's a navigation system. We call it the ASE: All Seeing Eye. We don't have windows here, so we use it to see where we're going.

KAREN
Unbelievable.

LITA
I must warn you. This thing goes fast. At least take a seat.

KAREN

Where are you taking me?

Shrugging, Lita places her hands on TWO BIORHYTHMIC
SENSORS, and the saucer takes off at such a breakneck speed,
that the momentum throws Karen against the wall.

LITA (CONT'D)

Told you to buckle up.

KAREN

Is this really a flying saucer?

LITA

Yup. It's built with UFO technology recovered from crashes.
The Air Force's been building them since the 50s. Ever heard of
Roswell?

Karen observes through the ASE how the saucer travels
smoothly through a network of dark CONCRETE TUNNELS.

KAREN

So, is that why you kidnapped Nathan? To steal more top secret
technology?

LITA

I'm afraid it's a lot more complicated than that.

Lita makes a sharp turn.

Still too proud to put on her seatbelt, Karen gets knocked down on her butt. This time, she gets up fuming and straps herself to a seat.

Lita looks at her out of the corner of her eye and holds back a grin.

KAREN
Alright, you made your point. Where is Nathan? I want to see him.

LITA
He got away.

KAREN
(frozen in disbelief)
He did not.

Lita nods affirmatively.

KAREN (CONT'D)
He would've called me.

LITA
Hasn't it ever occurred to you that he might not tell you every-thing?

At first, Karen appears confused and, for a brief moment, she doesn't know what to say, but soon she thinks of a comeback.

KAREN
He *has* to keep certain things from me. It's the nature of his job.

LITA
I don't mean those kind of secrets. Well, actually yes, those too, but I was referring to something more ... personal?

KAREN
What are you talking about?

LITA
Well, take your parents for instance. Has he ever told you who they were, or why you can't remember anything about your past?

KAREN
(irritated)
My real parents are dead, so whatever you think you know about me, you haven't got a clue.

LITA
See, that's where you're wrong.

KAREN
You've been stalking me, haven't you?

LITA

Maybe.

(pauses)

Or maybe not.

KAREN

When did Nathan escape?

LITA

Right before the explosion.

KAREN

So that's why you bombed the temple? To get back at Nathan?

LITA

(confused)

We had nothing to do with the explosion.

KAREN

We? Who is *we*?

LITA

You'll meet my boys soon enough. They'll tell you the same thing I'm telling you. The man you call "dad" was long gone by the time the temple exploded.

KAREN

How does bombing the temple benefit you guys?

LITA

It doesn't. We were after the Colonel. Not the temple.

KAREN

So you're saying there was no bomb?

LITA

That's right.

Karen thinks for a moment.

KAREN

(thinking out loud)

Dr. Kahn was on to something then.

LITA

What did you say?

KAREN

Nothing. I have to go. Let me out of here.

LITA

Captain, this place is a maze. Do you want to get lost?

KAREN

That's my problem. Now take me back to the shaft where you
picked me up and let me out.

LITA
Fine. I was just trying to help.

Lita reprograms the saucer to travel backwards in the opposite direction. After a few minutes, the saucer comes to a full stop.

Karen unstraps herself.

KAREN
I don't need your help. Just let me out of here.

LITA
If they find you, and they will sooner or later—

KAREN
Who is *they*?

LITA
(sighs hesitantly)
The same ones responsible for the disappearance of the rangers.

KAREN
How do you know about that? That's classified information.

LITA
I also know that you're looking for a way into the underground base below the temple.

KAREN

The facility is a base? You mean as in a military base?

Lita nods affirmatively.

KAREN (CONT'D)

I knew it! You're with the Libertador, aren't you?

Lita pulls a lever on a panel, and we hear the LOUD HISS of
air as it begins escaping from a vacuum-sealed IRIS VALVE
HATCH on the saucer's underbelly.

LITA

Actually, it's the other way around. He's with *us*. We're an
interplanetary force that has been around for thousands of years.
(pointing at the black sun insignia on her jacket)
The Sub Galactic League.

Sensing Karen's skepticism, Lita enters a code on A KEYPAD,
and AN AUTOMATIC DOOR on the wall slides open to reveal
A WHOLE ARSENAL OF HI-TECH WEAPONS.

Karen can hardly believe her eyes.

Lita takes out A FLASH GUN and hands it to her.

LITA (CONT'D)

Here, take this.

KAREN

(gasping)

What for?

LITA

Trust me, you'll need it. You insist on going out there on your own? I'll say a prayer for you.

Taking one last puzzled look at Lita, Karen accepts the flash gun reluctantly.

KAREN

Why would you give me a weapon? I just tried to kill you.

LITA

Like I said before, Captain. You're going to need it.

KAREN

So ... I'm not your prisoner, then?

LITA

Of course not. I already told you. I was just trying to help.

KAREN

Whatever. I still can't trust you.

LITA

Good luck then.

Doubting herself, Karen puts the gun in her backpack and exits slowly through the hatch that just opened. Lita closes the hatch, then, as the saucer takes off, she puts on A HEADSET.

LITA (CONT'D)
Caesar, come in. Do you read me?
(waits for response)
I made contact with her. She's down in the tunnels. Bay 6.
Sector 13.
(in an ominous tone)
She's all alone down there.

INT. TUNNELS - DAY

Moments later, Karen has ventured deep into the network of tunnels and is wandering cautiously down a pitch-dark tunnel.

Using her helmet light, she explores her surroundings with the help of A PORTABLE GPS LOCATOR and A UCM (ULTRA-SONIC CAVE MAPPING) DEVICE about the size of a cell phone.

Attached to her wrist with a Velcro strap, the UCM has a monitor that displays ultrasonic images of the tunnels, mapping large sections of the network at one time.

From time to time, Karen refers back to the printout with the blueprints she seized in Colombia, trying to find the one tunnel that leads to the underground base.

As she explores one of the tunnels, she suddenly stumbles across A SET OF LARGE TRACKS with THREE BIG TOES.

She kneels down to examine them and notices they ARE FRESHLY MADE. She gets back up on her feet and looks around, not sure of where to turn.

Just then, A FLEETING SHADOW passes quickly behind her. Karen turns around but sees nothing, so she immediately pulls out the laser gun Lita gave her.

KAREN
Is someone there?

No response.

KAREN (CONT'D)
Hello?

Nothing.

She backtracks slowly in the direction where the shadow passed, pointing the gun upwards, ready to shoot.

As she draws near A T INTERSECTION with tunnels on both sides, THE SOUND of BREATHING stops her dead in her tracks. She holds still, listening intently, her body shaking as steam billows out of her mouth.

The breathing gradually becomes A DEEP, VICIOUS SNARL.

Karen takes a couple steps back, gripping the gun tightly with both hands and pointing it forward. Hearing the snarling coming closer, she moves further backwards, now a few yards away from the intersection.

KAREN (CONT'D)
(breathing hard)
Who's there?

Just then, she hears LOUD STEPS coming from the tunnel to the left of the intersection.

She retreats a little more, gun in hand, then watches in shock as A HUGE SILHOUETTE emerges from the shadows.

It's too dark for Karen to see it clearly but the one thing she notices is that the figure is much too tall and bulky to be human.

As her eyes adjust to the darkness, she is suddenly able to make out its HUGE, GLOWING, RED EYES and VERTICAL SLIT PUPILS like those of A SNAKE.

The moment the creature takes a step towards her, Karen takes a sharp U-turn and makes a dash in the opposite direction as she realizes there are at least FIVE GIGANTIC CREATURES coming her way.

She shoots at a couple of them, her teeth chattering as she hears the GHASTLY, HIGH-PITCHED SHRIEKS they let out as they get hit.

While she succeeds at killing about half of them, the remaining ones manage to avoid the beams and get so close, they're practically breathing down her neck.

Karen speeds up and runs as fast as her legs will carry her, glancing often at the UCM monitor to see where she is going.

Yet, with the creatures so close on her tail, she overlooks A DEAD END as she whips around a corner that leads to a:

INT. SHAFT - CONTINUOUS

Horrified, Karen learns that this is yet another VERTICAL SHAFT, only this one is A CAVERNOUS PIT, partially UNDER CONSTRUCTION and with no bottom in sight like the first one.

Her momentum doesn't give her enough time to stop, so she slips feet first over the edge and nearly falls, accidentally dropping the flash gun. At the last minute, she grabs on and winds up cliff-hanging from the edge by a single hand.

As she struggles to grab the edge with her other hand, she hears
the approaching footsteps of the creatures, now almost on top of
her.

Just then, she sees A BRIGHT NEON GLOW flashing around
the corner from where she came.

Along with the glow, she recognizes the SOUND of FLASH
GUNS being fired. The creatures SCREECH LOUDLY, and
soon AN UTTER SILENCE swallows up the chaos.

Karen makes several attempts to lift herself up over the edge
until A HUMAN HAND suddenly grabs hers and swiftly pulls
her up.

Once on firm ground, Karen finds herself staring into the eyes
of her archnemesis, EL LIBERTADOR, who wears A JACKET
with A BLACK SUN INSIGNIA like the one Lita had on.

KAREN
What the hell?

Standing beside him, we see Marcus, the man we saw at the
square stalking Nathan. He also wears the same silver jacket.
Raising his chin in a challenging gesture, Marcus stands next to
the Libertador like a watch dog.

Deeply confused, Karen scrutinizes the Libertador, her eyes full of questions. She observes he has DEEP CLAW MARKS on his leg, but the blood in them has already dried up, showing evidence that they're not freshly made.

MARCUS
(to Libertador)
Come on, Caesar. We gotta get out of here.

KAREN
(to Libertador)
Your real name... is Caesar?

CAESAR
That's what they call me.

KAREN
Why did you help me?

CAESAR
They're my enemies, too.

KAREN
But ... don't you know who I am?

CAESAR
Of course I do.
(a pause)
That's *why* I helped you.

He turns around to leave, and so does Marcus.

KAREN
(frustrated)
Wait, what? How can you help me if I've been hunting you
down for years?

Caesar stops walking and turns back around to face her.

CAESAR
We don't have time to talk about that right now.

MARCUS
Caesar, they're coming.

KAREN
(suspicious, looking around)
Who's coming?

CAESAR
(to Karen)
Your people. They're looking for you.

KAREN
I'm not going anywhere until you talk to me.

CAESAR
Goodbye, Captain. We'll meet again soon, I hope.

KAREN
But ... how will I find you?

MARCUS
Caesar—

CAESAR
Find the Black Sun.

Something dawns on Karen as she hears these words, so she produces the printout with the scanned blueprints on it and shows it to Caesar.

KAREN
Is that what these blueprints are for? To locate the Black Sun?

Caesar nods, but doesn't have time to linger because Marcus pulls him along and forces him to keep going. Fascinated, Karen watches the two men as they disappear into the darkness beyond.

Nervously glancing behind her, she turns off her helmet light and puts on a pair of NIGHT-VISION GOGGLES. She delves into the shadows, silently following after them.

EXT. GRANITE MOUNTAINS - NIGHT

Up on the surface that night, NUMEROUS POLICE CARS

surround the MOUNTAIN VAULT along with K-9 UNITS, PARAMEDICS, A FIRETRUCK, and A CIVILIAN SEARCH & RESCUE TEAM.

As the crews spread out all across the area, their dogs searching the mountains, A K-9 OFFICER and his GERMAN SHEPHERD hasten out of the woods and head for the canyon where Karen left her dirt bike.

EXT. CANYON - CONTINUOUS

Standing by the bike, we see NATHAN. He appears healthy and unscathed, his uniform impeccably clean.

The K-9 officer walks up to him.

K-9 OFFICER

Colonel, I think we may have found something.

EXT. CREVICE - NIGHT

Moments later, Nathan and the K-9 officer arrive at the crevice through which Karen descended earlier.

SEVERAL OFFICERS have gathered there as well, illuminating the area with their FLASHLIGHTS.

As they see Nathan approaching, they step aside to let him get by.

The K-9 officer points at THE ANCHOR Karen drilled into the rock.

Nathan crouches down to examine THE ROPE attached to the anchor.

K-9 OFFICER
My dog picked up her scent on the rope. It's definitely hers.

Nathan follows the rope through the crevice to see where it leads.

INT. CAVERN - NIGHT

Meanwhile, Karen secretly follows Marcus and Caesar as they travel down a misty cavern.

Even though the dense white mist makes it difficult for her to see, Karen is still able to make out a series of STRANGE MARKINGS on the wall.

Careful not to lose sight of the men, she slows down to examine the markings and notices they're ANCIENT HIEROGLYPHICS.

Above them, she discerns a HAND-PAINTED ILLUSTRATION depicting A FEATHERED SERPENT with a crested head and scaly skin. Its arms and hind legs have claws like an eagle's talons, and it stands up like a human.

To Karen's surprise, the creature's eyes have VERTICAL SLIT PUPILS, just like the ones who chased her back in the tunnels.

In its right hand, it carries a SCEPTER, atop of which is A BLACK SUN similar to her birthmark.

A GROUP OF HUMANS are portrayed kneeling down before the being, as though worshipping it.

Strangely, as soon as she sees the cave painting, Karen's nose starts BLEEDING again.

Suddenly, in the distance, she hears the approaching SOUND of MEN RUNNING, accompanied by DOGS BARKING.

Karen hesitates, looking at Caesar and Marcus as they move farther and farther away from her. She takes a step towards them, but then something she hears makes her stop and look the other way.

INT. TUNNELS - CONTINUOUS

It's Nathan, calling out to her as he leads the rescue team down the labyrinth where Karen was earlier.

NATHAN

Karen! Karen!

INT. CAVERN - CONTINUOUS

Karen recognizes his voice.

NATHAN (O.S.)

Karen!

KAREN

Nathan? Is that you?

She searches for Caesar and Marcus, but they're already so far ahead, she can no longer see them.

Finally, making up her mind, she decides to head back in the direction of Nathan's voice.

INT. TUNNELS - CONTINUOUS

Karen tracks Nathan down in the tunnels until she finds her way back to him. The moment she spots him, she runs towards him with a bright smile on her face.

As Nathan sees Karen approaching, he signals for the team to stop.

NATHAN
(to team)
Wait here.

He advances forward towards her, leaving the team behind. As he draws closer to her, he opens his arms to hold her, smiling ear to ear.

Karen hugs him.

KAREN
Oh, Dad, I'm so glad you're okay. I was so worried.

NATHAN
You shouldn't have come down here, sweetheart. It's too dangerous.

Just then, Karen realizes that he looks perfectly fine, as if nothing had happened. Her smile fades as she becomes suspicious.

KAREN
Why didn't you tell me you'd escaped?

NATHAN
(reading her)
I called the Chief. He told me you'd come looking for me. I've been trying to reach you on your cell phone.

KAREN
(not buying it)
Where were you during the explosion?

NATHAN
What kind of question is that, honey?

KAREN
I called your cell phone several times—

NATHAN
Why are you using that tone with me, Karen?

KAREN
Please tell me.

NATHAN
(suspicious)
Who have you been talking to?

KAREN
No one in particular.

NATHAN
Who?

KAREN
Why won't you answer my question?

NATHAN
I'll answer after you tell me who you've been talking to.

KAREN
Something here doesn't add up. I can see it for myself. No one
has to tell me anything.

NATHAN
What are you suggesting?

KAREN
Nothing. I just need to know—

NATHAN
(upset, interrupting her)
Listen to me, Karen. This is the last time I'm going to ask you
this. Who have you been talking to?

She swallows hard, hesitating for a moment.

KAREN
People.

NATHAN
What kind of people?

KAREN
I answered your question, now please answer mine.

NATHAN

That's not an answer. I want names.

KAREN

What about my question? Why won't you answer me?

NATHAN

I said I want names first.

KAREN

How come I don't know anything about my real parents?

NATHAN

(thrown off)

What does this have to do with—

KAREN

And what about my childhood? Why
can't I remember anything?

NATHAN

You're going to give me those names, Karen.

KAREN

I want to know the truth.

NATHAN

Fine. You want the truth? Here it is.

(emphatically)

He's out to destroy you and everything you hold dear.

KAREN

If you mean the Libertador, you're seriously mistaken. He just
saved my life!

Nathan looks at her in shock. Shaking his head in disapproval,
he remains silent.

KAREN (CONT'D)

Why would he save me, Nathan? If he knows all this time I've
been trying to put him away and have him executed?

NATHAN

He's brainwashed you. You should know better, Karen. It's
the terrorist cult mentality I've always warned you about, and
you're falling for it!

KAREN

Why is he after you?

NATHAN

He's out to kill us both. Don't you see? He's pitting us against
each other. It's the oldest trick in the book. Divide and conquer.

KAREN

Then why would he save my life?

Nathan sighs, making a decision.

NATHAN
Karen ... I've never wanted to tell you this before, but now you
have forced me.

KAREN
(confused)
What?

NATHAN
When you were a child, you ... you killed a man.

She takes a step back, shaking her head in disbelief.

NATHAN (CONT'D)
That's why I had to come pick you up at the hospital. That's
why I've been so secretive all these years. To protect you.

KAREN
How did it happen?

NATHAN
A lab tech at the ER tried to draw your blood, so you killed him
because you felt threatened.

KAREN
But how—

NATHAN

You would've been tried as an adult if I hadn't interfered.

KAREN

So why *did* you?

NATHAN

Because I saw potential in that little girl. She was all alone in
the world, and I knew I could turn things around for her.

KAREN

But why can't I remember?

NATHAN

Because I helped you block it. I knew it would've marked you
for life if I didn't. It would have ruined you, Karen. I did it to
protect you, to give you a fighting chance.

KAREN

It doesn't make any sense. You taught me yourself that I have to
face things for what they are.

NATHAN
(snapping)
I've explained enough already. I want those names now.

KAREN

I can't.

NATHAN

Alright, then you leave me with no choice. You have 24 hours
to bring the Libertador to me. 24 hours, Karen.

KAREN

What makes you think I can get to him?

NATHAN

He's the person you've been talking to. Him and his terrorist
guerrillas.

KAREN

What do you want from him? Tell me the truth.

NATHAN

He's a thug, wanted for treason. You've always known this. I
don't understand why you're having doubts now. Do you want
to wind up like him?

KAREN

You're hiding things from me. Do you really think I'm that
stupid?

NATHAN

Twenty-four hours or else, Karen.

The wheels turning in her head, she looks into his eyes, antici-
pating his next move.

KAREN
You're done lying to me.

Right as Nathan lifts up his hand to summon the team, Karen spins around and takes off running in the opposite direction.

NATHAN
Karen! Get back here! You got nowhere to go!

The K-9 officer approaches him.

K-9 OFFICER
Do you want us to go after her, sir?

His face red with anger, Nathan thinks for a moment. He takes a deep breath and composes himself.

NATHAN
Let her run all she wants. She won't get very far.

K-9 OFFICER
But, sir—

NATHAN
I want the entire rescue team back up on the surface now. As soon as you're all out, seal the crevice. I want surveillance there 24/7, starting right now. Once the crevice is sealed, no one gets in or out without my authorization, understood?

CUT TO:

INT. CAVERN – NIGHT

Having found her way back into the cavern with the hieroglyphics, Karen makes sure no one has followed her.

She then ventures down a narrow passageway and heads in the direction of the spot where she last saw Caesar and Marcus.

When she reaches the opening on the other side, she comes to a screeching halt as she sees that the ground slopes down into A NARROW CHASM.

The bottom of the chasm lies about 100 feet below where she stands. Karen looks down and finds a rope ladder that leads to the bottom. She carefully climbs down the ladder and ends up in the:

INT. RUINS OF AN ANCIENT CITY - CONTINUOUS

The structure of the buildings resemble those of Aztec and Mayan cities. As KAREN approaches the entrance to the ruins, she runs into A TALL WATCHTOWER with steps like a pyramid.

She draws closer to the tower and realizes A BEARDED MAN is watching her from above. This is the SAME MAN we saw posing as Lita's paramedic partner back at Temple Square.

KAREN
Hello?

As the man steps down from the tower, Karen notices he's wearing the same SILVER JACKET as the Sub Galactic League.

He pulls out a FLASH GUN just like the one Lita gave Karen earlier and points it at her head, his face devoid of emotion. Karen throws her hands up in the air.

KAREN (CONT'D)
Whoa! Hey, wait, I'm unarmed.

He digs the gun barrel into her back and pushes her forward, forcing her to walk.

KAREN (CONT'D)
Wait, just tell me where to find the Black Sun and I'll leave.

The man stops as soon as he hears what Karen has just said.

KAREN (CONT'D)
Caesar's waiting for me there. You know Caesar and Lita, right?

Still saying nothing, the man grabs the backpack away from her and checks its contents.

In it he finds her wallet, so he pulls it out, opens it and finds her USAF badge.

He scoffs with derision, putting her wallet in his pocket. Then, he shoves her hard toward the inside of the city ruins, leaving her backpack behind on the ground.

KAREN (CONT'D)
No, please, it's not what you think. I need my backpack. Why can't you call the League? They're the ones who led me here.

INT. RUINS - NIGHT

The bearded man continues to give Karen the silent treatment while pushing her forward into what appears to be the main avenue of the city ruins.

Meanwhile, Karen observes her surroundings with great curiosity. The place seems to be the POST-APOCALYPTIC remnant of an ancient civilization that evidently endured some type of CATASTROPHE in the distant past.

As the bearded man presses the barrel of the flash gun into Karen's back, he leads her towards:

INT. A COBBLESTONE TRAIL - CONTINUOUS

The trail is lined with MAKESHIFT TENTS on either side of it.

As Karen and her captor go past the tents, the INHABITANTS poke out their heads through the doors and windows to steal glances at Karen.

There are ENTIRE FAMILIES dressed in PRIMITIVE CLOTHING. They almost look like a PREHISTORIC CLAN OF CAVE PEOPLE.

In the far distance, Karen spots a vast open space with A GEOTHERMAL POWER PLANT AND STEAM GENERATORS.

Beyond the power plant is A LARGE HYDROPONIC VEGETABLE PLANTATION with SODIUM LAMPS.

After a long walk of shame, the man leads Karen into what appears to be the:

INT. TOWN SQUARE - CONTINUOUS

FURS, FEATHERS, BONES and other trinkets are piled up on WOODEN TABLES. It looks like A MARKET PLACE for people to barter.

As the bearded man forces Karen towards the center of the square, A MALE and TWO FEMALES dressed in furs bolt up from behind a CRUMBLED STONE WALL.

The male picks up A WOODEN STAFF and advances menacingly towards Karen, so she puts her hands in the air.

Strangely enough, the man stares at her like he's afraid of her.

The bearded man keeps pushing Karen forward while the cave man stalks silently behind her, pointing the staff at her.

Karen keeps walking, looking over her shoulder often.
As the two men lead her past several DECAYED BUILDINGS, Karen sees HEADS popping out left and right, PEOPLE of all ages, including YOUNG CHILDREN, all of them the product of a culture seemingly gone back to tribalism.

CUT TO:

A set of WOODEN DOUBLE DOORS flies open from the outside.

WIDER TO REVEAL:

INT. BASEMENT - CONTINUOUS

As the doors let in some light, we see it is the bearded man that just opened them. He grips Karen by the arm and thrusts her headfirst into the basement below, then shuts the doors again.

Karen screams as she lands hard on the rugged ground and immediately coils up into a fetal position, writhing and groaning in pain.

MALE VOICE (O.S.)
Who's there?

Startled, Karen flips on her helmet light and sits up. She is greatly relieved to discover TWO ARMY RANGERS sitting propped up against the back wall of the basement. Their uniforms dirty, and their faces pale, both rangers appear worn out.

SERGEANT JIMENEZ, the one who just spoke, is Mexican-American, mid 30s. He covers his face as Karen shines the light on him.

KAREN
Sorry.

The other RANGER is unresponsive and delirious. He just babbles some nonsense from time to time and appears to be too far gone.

SERGEANT JIMENEZ
(to Karen)
Are you Search and Rescue?

KAREN
No, I'm Captain Samuels, Air Force Black Ops, and you are?

SERGEANT JIMENEZ

Sergeant Jimenez, Army Rangers. Were you sent here to find us?

KAREN

No, but I did hear about a detachment that went missing. What happened to the rest of your team?

SERGEANT JIMENEZ

We're all that's left.

Karen examines the wounded ranger and notices he has BLOODY CLAW MARKS on his legs and arms. They are similar to the ones she saw on Caesar, but the ones on the ranger are smaller and severely infected.

KAREN

Who did this to him? It wasn't the people out there, or was it?

SERGEANT JIMENEZ

No, he got attacked back in the tunnels.

KAREN

By an animal?

SERGEANT JIMENEZ

I don't know what those things are. They look like—

KAREN

Reptiles?

SERGEANT JIMENEZ

You've seen them, too?

KAREN

Yes, unfortunately ... What are they?

SERGEANT JIMENEZ

They're the strangest creatures I've ever seen. They call them reptilians.

KAREN

What do you know about them?

SERGEANT JIMENEZ

Not much. The scientists in our team kept everything to themselves, but I overheard a thing or two.

KAREN

What did you hear?

SERGEANT JIMENEZ

Apparently, they're an evolved species of reptilian hybrids. Half reptile, half human. That's why they're bipedal. They're really powerful predators. We humans don't stand a chance against them.

KAREN

Are they the ones who caused the explosion?

SERGEANT JIMENEZ

That's what we were sent here for. To find out what caused it, but, as you can see, we got attacked by the reptilians first and, then, those of us who survived got captured by those lunatics out there.

KAREN

What happened to the scientists in your team? They were Dr. Kahn's people, right?

SERGEANT JIMENEZ

Yes. They all got killed off. One by one. Torn apart by the creatures.

KAREN

How many reptilians would you say there are? I killed a bunch of them up in the tunnels, but I'm pretty sure there's more.

SERGEANT JIMENEZ

There's a hell of a lot more, alright. An entire army I'd say.

KAREN

I found some strange paintings up there in the caverns above the ruins. It looks like the reptilians have been here since prehistoric times. The cave paintings show humans worshipping them.

SERGEANT JIMENEZ

I really can't tell you much. All I know is that the nomads out there are scared shitless of them.

KAREN

How do you know they're nomads?

SERGEANT JIMENEZ

I dunno. They look like nomads to me. More like cannibals, actually. Wouldn't be surprised if they were keeping us here to cook us for dinner later on.

KAREN

We can't just sit around waiting to find out then. We've got to find a way out of here. Are you able to walk?

SERGEANT JIMENEZ

I'm really weak but I could probably manage. I'm not going to leave my comrade behind, though.

She lowers her voice so the other ranger won't hear.

KAREN

I don't think he's going to make it for much longer. The infection in his leg has probably spread all over his body by now.

SERGEANT JIMENEZ

Still! What am I going to tell his family if I make it out alive?

That I left his body behind to rot in some basement?

KAREN
We can give him a proper burial right here. I'll help you dig a hole in the ground.

SERGEANT JIMENEZ
Absolutely not, lady. I'm not going to do that to my friend. You have no idea what he and I have been through together. I'm not leaving him behind.

KAREN
Alright, fine. I'll go see if I can get help then.

SERGEANT JIMENEZ
(scoffs cynically)
Yeah, sure. That's if those cavemen let you out of here. I don't mean to burst your bubble, but that ain't going to happen any-time soon if they got anything to say about it.

Karen sighs in frustration and starts looking around.

SERGEANT JIMENEZ (CONT'D)
What are you doing?

KAREN
There must be another way out of here.

SERGEANT JIMENEZ

Believe me. I spent hours looking. The only way out of here is
through those double doors.

Unwilling to take his word for it, Karen tries to get up but, as
she supports her weight on her left arm, she screams out in
agony.

KAREN

Dammit! I must have dislocated my arm when I landed.

SERGEANT JIMENEZ

Face it, Captain. We're probably looking at our final resting
place, so you might want to say your peace right about now.

KAREN

I'm not going to lay down and die. Besides, all I need to do is
find the Black Sun, and they'll let us go.

SERGEANT JIMENEZ
(perking up)
The Black Sun?

KAREN
Yes! Do you know where it is?

SERGEANT JIMENEZ
No, but ...

(pausing to remember)

Now that you mention it, Kahn's scientists were looking for it, too. It's that damn explosive crystal they kept going on and on about.

Karen's jaw practically drops in disbelief.`

KAREN

Wait a second. Are you saying the crystal is the Black Sun?

SERGEANT JIMENEZ

That's what the scientists said, but you never heard it from me.

KAREN

OMG, Sarge, why didn't you tell me that before?

SERGEANT JIMENEZ

Well, for once, you never asked, plus I'm not really supposed to talk about it. My team was sworn to secrecy before we were dispatched.

KAREN

(whispering to herself)

So that's why Nathan's after Caesar then.

SERGEANT JIMENEZ

What did you say?

Karen shakes her head in dismay, her mind somewhere else.

KAREN

Nothing. Just, uh, thinking out loud, that's all.

SERGEANT JIMENEZ

Okay, so would you mind telling me how this Black Sun can get
us out of here?

Just then, the double doors fly open again.

Both Karen and the sergeant snap their heads with anticipation.

It's the bearded man.

He lowers A LADDER through the opening and starts climbing
down with A LONG IRON CHAIN rolled around his shoulder.

As the bearded man turns his back on them to climb down,
Karen exchanges furtive glances with the sergeant, gesturing for
him to move closer to the ladder.

The sergeant opens his eyes wide, frantically shaking his head
no.

Wasting no time, Karen darts toward the ladder and begins rat-
tling it, trying to make the bearded man fall.

This pisses off the bearded man, so, out of nowhere, he does a backflip in midair and lands on his feet, ready to attack.

His SUPERHUMAN MOVES are reminiscent of Lita's.

KAREN
Oops!

As the man goes for the chains, Karen dives on top of the sergeant in an attempt to protect him, but the bearded man is much too fast for her.

Growling with rage, he singlehandedly grabs Karen by the neck and chokeslams her.

Karen CRIES OUT in agony as a stream of blood gushes out of her mouth. She quickly tries to get up, but the man wraps the chains around her neck and starts to strangle her.

Karen coughs, desperately gasping for air, but the man only tightens the chains more, all the while with a sadistic sneer on his lips.

Suddenly, out of nowhere, Sergeant Jimenez leaps up and kicks the man in the lower back, then tries to lock in a sleeper hold around his neck, but the bearded man spins around, flings Karen to the ground and seizes Jimenez by the collar with both hands.

While Karen lands on her knees and struggles to catch her breath, the bearded man lifts Jimenez up in the air and swings him around over his head, then hurls him right smack against the wall.

By now, Karen has mildly recovered from the attack, but she remains on the ground, crouching like a lioness ready to pounce.

KAREN
Hey buddy, look over here!

The bearded man charges at her, bellowing like a bull. But, right as he's about to strike her with the full weight of the chains, Karen dodges the blow and jabs her knee into his crotch.

The man doubles up in pain, SQUEALING.

KAREN
(smiling triumphantly)
Works every time.

Without hesitation, she snatches the chains away from him and repeatedly strikes him across the face with them until the blood spurts out of his nose and he's down on the ground.

Meanwhile, Jimenez comes to her aid and kicks the man while he's down. Once they've worn him out, they wrap the chains around his torso and arms and leave him lying there. Next, they proceed to carry the other ranger out.

INT. RUINS - CONTINUOUS

Karen and Jimenez emerge from the basement with a nearly dead ranger in tow. But, just when they think they are home free, they find themselves surrounded by AN ANGRY MOB OF CAVE PEOPLE ready to stone them.

DISSOLVE TO:

EXT. HILL AIR FORCE BASE - UTAH - DAY

A helicopter lands on the deck, and Larson climbs out of it. He dashes into the base escorted by an MP SQUAD.

INT. OFFICE - HILL AFB - CONTINUOUS

Nathan is sitting at his desk when the chief walks in and salutes him.

Without getting up from his chair, Nathan gestures for Larson to sit down and it is clear by the look on his face that he's seething.

NATHAN
How many years have we known each other, Larson? At least ten?

LARSON

Sir, I understand you're upset, but I can explain.

Nathan slams his fist on the desk.

NATHAN

I don't want an explanation. I thought I could trust you.

LARSON

Of course you can trust me, sir.

NATHAN

She's the daughter I never had, goddammit! Why would you let her go without my permission?

LARSON

We weren't sure where you were, sir. She was worried sick, and I ... I honestly thought you were dead.

NATHAN
(shaking his head disapprovingly)
I entrusted you with my most prized possession. My only child!

LARSON

She's extremely headstrong, sir.

NATHAN

Are you saying you can't control her?

LARSON

No, sir, of course not. I can fix this. Just give me one day.
That's all I ask. One day, and I'll bring her back safe and sound.

NATHAN

She's gone. It's too late. The Libertador's got her brainwashed.

LARSON

She's too smart for that. I can reason with her. Just tell me
where you last saw her, and I'll bring her back.

NATHAN

She's down in the tunnels somewhere. I got no way to reach her.

LARSON

I will find her for you, sir. That's a promise.

NATHAN

I'm not sure she wants to be found.

LARSON

If it's the last thing I do, I will bring her back.

Nathan shakes his head no and slams his hand on his desk, looking like a truck just ran over him.

NATHAN

You have no idea what you're getting into.

LARSON

What makes you say that, sir?

NATHAN

Well, for one, your loyalties are divided.

LARSON

What do you mean?

NATHAN

You say you want to go down there and bring Karen back, but
the question is, are you doing it for me ... or for her?

LARSON

For both of you, of course. I believe it's in her best interest to
come back to you, sir.

NATHAN

I know you care about her wellbeing, Larson. I know you do.
And I appreciate that very much, but at the same time it makes
me wonder if you'd take her side.

LARSON

Take her side how? She'd never go against you, sir. You're the
only father she's ever known.

NATHAN

What if I told you she's not the same person anymore? This past couple of days she's been down there has really changed her. She's been talking to the Libertador, and that's done things to her mind. It's made her ask questions she's never asked before.

LARSON

She's just confused, I'm sure, but I can convince her. She always listens to me.

NATHAN

Let's say for instance, if she were to tell you things, things that might be compelling enough to doubt everything you've been taught. What would you do then?

LARSON

I can't imagine anything she could possibly tell me that would make me question you, sir. And, besides, I'm a man of my word. I will fulfill my duty at all costs. I'm giving you my word of honor that I will bring her back. I will keep my promise or die trying.

NATHAN

Even if it means you lose her in the end?

LARSON

I wouldn't lose her. I'd never let anything happen to her. I'm going down there to rescue her and bring her back safely. No harm will come to her as long as she's with me. You can count on that.

NATHAN

What I mean, Larson, is losing her trust, her friendship. Whatever bond exists between the two of you, I know it goes beyond
the work you do together.

LARSON

(swallowing hard)

With all due respect, sir, I have never done anything inappropri-
ate if that's what you're suggesting. I have all the respect in the
world for her as my right hand and comrade in arms. There's
nothing more.

NATHAN

I know you'd never cross the line, of course. That's not what I
meant. But you do have to admit that you're fond of her. After
all, she is a very attractive girl. She's around you all the time,
and it must be tempting to say the least—

LARSON

(exploding)

Stop, sir, please stop! It's nothing like that, I assure you.

NATHAN

Oh, Larson, Larson. I know you're wise beyond your years, and
I greatly admire you for that, but you cannot deceive me. I'm
not blind. I know Karen and you *fancy* each other, so to speak.

Deeply embarrassed, Larson turns his back on Nathan.

LARSON

Please don't say that, sir.

NATHAN

It's beyond words. Clearly, neither one of you has acted on it, but it's constantly there, in the back of both your minds. Latent. Suppressed, if you will. But it's very real, and those kinds of feelings can be quite intoxicating. Debilitating, even.

LARSON

This conversation is making me feel really uncomfortable, sir. I don't know what you're trying to do here.

NATHAN

It's simple. I'm trying to find out if I can trust you enough to send you down there to retrieve her.

LARSON

I don't know what else to say to convince you that yes, you can. I will risk my own life if that's what it takes to bring her back.

NATHAN

What I fear, Larson, is that, under the right circumstances, during a moment of weakness perhaps, your feelings for her could betray you.

LARSON

Never, sir. I'd never give into it. No matter what the circumstances are, my duty will always come first.

NATHAN

But if your duty is to rescue her, she could easily manipulate
you. Especially if she, too, is aware of your feelings for her.

LARSON

(gasps)

Has she ...

(clears his throat nervously)

mentioned anything to you, sir?

NATHAN

(laughs sarcastically)

Oh, no, no, of course not, but if *I* have noticed it, who's to say
she herself hasn't as well?

LARSON

She'd never manipulate me like that, sir. She and I trust each
other with our lives. Karen ...

(shakes head in frustration)

I mean ... Captain Samuels is a woman of honor. She's just as
committed to her duty as I am.

NATHAN

What if I told you that that's no longer the case? Those terrorists
have twisted her mind. She's questioning everything I've ever
taught her now. I'm telling you, Larson, we are dealing with a

very delicate situation here. One that could go very wrong, very fast.

LARSON

I understand your concern, sir. Let's say this is a phenomenon similar to the Patti Hearst case. We can still deprogram her after we rescue her. We can keep her contained for some time if it's necessary. I've dealt with those types of issues in the past.

NATHAN

Which brings me back to my concern about *you*. The work you did for the CIA left you deeply scarred. The evaluations you received weren't favorable at all.

LARSON

Yes, sir, it was a rough assignment, I admit it, but I recovered from it. I went right back to work after I got out of the hospital. If you read my doctor's reports, you'll see that I complied with all his discharge instructions and I've been perfectly fine ever since.

Nathan fiddles with a pen as the wheels turn in his head.

NATHAN

My fear is that, when it comes down to it, you might have to make a choice between Karen and your loyalty to your country. And, to be completely honest, I'm not sure you're prepared to handle that kind of pressure.

LARSON

There's no question in my mind that my loyalties lie with you
and my country, sir. No matter what happens.

NATHAN

Even if she's persuasive enough to make you doubt me?

LARSON

Sir, if you authorize me for this mission, I will prove beyond the
shadow of a doubt that my loyalty to you is unwavering.

NATHAN

I'd have to permanently reassign her if you do succeed in bring-
ing her back. You understand that, don't you?

LARSON
(taken aback)
So you're saying ... I may never see her again?

Nathan puts his hand on the chief's shoulder.

NATHAN
(in a patronizing tone)
It would be for your own good, son.

Larson clenches his jaw and balls up his fists as he sinks into a
restless silence. He debates with himself. Then, after a moment,
a look of resigned determination appears on his face.

LARSON

I will respect your decision, sir. Regardless of what it is. Just
let me bring her back.

DISSOLVE TO:

INT. VALLEY FIELD - NIGHT

Later that night, Karen and the two Rangers are chained to a
stake in the middle of A VAST, DESERTED FIELD.

Nestled at the base of amazingly tall rock walls full of CARVED
PATTERNS, the field is a valley located just outside the city
ruins.

KAREN

I don't like it here. It's way too quiet.

SERGEANT JIMENEZ

Yeah, tell me about it.

KAREN

You see those carvings on the walls over there?
(gesturing with her head)
It's the same serpent man I saw in the cavern.

SERGEANT JIMENEZ

If I didn't know any better, I'd say this is the prehistoric version of a coliseum.

KAREN

Hopefully they're just going to torture us for information.

SERGEANT JIMENEZ

(chuckling darkly)

Sure, think positive. What have you got to lose, right?

KAREN

We're going to be okay.

SERGEANT JIMENEZ

No, seriously. Where did the cannibals go? Aren't they supposed to be the spectators?

KAREN

(ticked off)

You're really not helping, Sarge. You may as well shut up if you're going to be saying shit like that.

SERGEANT JIMENEZ

Aren't you a little curious about why they put us out here?

KAREN

Yeah. But so what if they're not here? They probably went back to their tents.

Right as she says that, Karen detects some movement to her right.

KAREN (CONT'D)
Wait, I think I just saw someone.

SERGEANT JIMENEZ
Where?

She snaps her head around and sees SOME HEADS popping out from behind a pile of rocks in the distance.

KAREN
Look! They're all hiding behind the rocks.

She continues to scan her surroundings and suddenly spots the bearded man as he emerges from the ruins carrying TWO POLE TORCHES.

With his nose newly bandaged, he takes long strides across the field and heads in Karen's direction.

SERGEANT JIMENEZ
Aaaargh, we're going to burn at the stake!

As the torchlight illuminates the field, Karen is shocked to discover that what she originally thought to be rocks are actually HUMAN CARCASSES. There are piles and piles of them scattered all over the field.

KAREN
(taking deep breaths)
Shhh, stay calm, Sarge, breathe.

SERGEANT JIMENEZ
(freaking out)
They're going to burn us alive!

But the bearded man only inserts the poles firmly into the ground, one on each side of the stake, and then turns around to leave. Then, something he sees stops him.

BEARDED MAN'S POV: Karen's birthmark. As he walks past her, he notices it for the first time under the torchlight.

He stares at it dumbfounded and, suddenly, right as he is examining it, A STRANGE NOISE is heard in the distance.

It's the OMINOUS SOUND of FLAPPING WINGS echoing through the field.

After hesitating for a few seconds, the bearded man disappears back into the darkness, a look of concern on his face.

SERGEANT JIMENEZ
Wait, where did he go?

KAREN
I don't know. I think he left.

Puzzled, Karen squints, trying to see past the area illuminated by the torches, but it's too dark.

KAREN (CONT'D)
Did you hear that?

SERGEANT JIMENEZ
What was it?

KAREN
Shhh, listen.

The SOUND grows closer and closer until, out of the shadows, A HUGE BEAST comes soaring across the depths and starts flying in circles above them.

Karen and the sergeant HOLLER at the top of their lungs when they behold the HIDEOUSNESS of what is headed their way.

At least two feet taller than the creatures Karen saw in the tunnels, the beast is A WINGED WHITE DRACO, an albino dragon-man with GARGOYLE WINGS similar to the one por-trayed in the carvings all around them.

He emits a terrifying HIGH-PITCHED SOUND accompanied

by A DEEP GROWL.

Karen closes her eyes as the draco claws his way through the chains and grabs the sergeant.

By the time Karen opens her eyes, the draco has already swallowed the sergeant whole.

Horrified, she frantically tries to help the other ranger up as he collapses, but she quickly realizes he's already dead.

Karen's legs buckle underneath her.

KAREN
(crying, whispering softly)
Sarge, I'm sorry! I'm so sorry!

Hearing Karen's voice, the beast lifts up his head to look into her eyes.

Karen holds his gaze and surrenders to her destiny, but, to her surprise, the draco doesn't move.

She's deeply confused when she notices the look in his eyes.

Woman and dragon stand facing each other for an instant when, suddenly, A TEAR rolls out of the draco's eye.

Karen swallows hard, never taking her eyes off the beast.

The draco slowly retreats one step, then another and another, until he turns around and takes off flying.

Entranced, Karen follows the draco with her eyes and watches him disappear into the darkness.

Then, shaking herself out of her trance, she realizes the cave people have come out of their hideouts.

Staring at her in silence, they gather round her like before, only this time, instead of capturing her, they FALL ON THEIR KNEES before her.

Dumbfounded, Karen notices that even the bearded man has bowed down.

BEARDED MAN
(humbly)
We owe you an apology.

CUT TO:

EXT. CREVICE - LITTLE COTTONWOOD CANYON - NIGHT

Chief Larson is dropped off by helicopter at the site where the rescue team is waiting on Karen. He comes equipped with all kinds of SPELUNKING GEAR. As he heads toward the crevice, A K-9 OFFICER stands in his way.

It is the same K-9 officer who received orders from Nathan to seal the crevice.

K-9 OFFICER
I'm sorry, sir, but this area is off limits.

CHIEF LARSON
I have a direct order from Colonel Preston to access this entrance. Please step aside.

The K-9 officer hesitates.

K-9 OFFICER
He told us no one could go in or out of here.

Larson shows him an official letter with the Hill Air Force Base seal and Nathan's signature.

CHIEF LARSON
I'm here to bring his daughter back. Let me through.

The moment the K-9 officer sees the letter, he motions for the rescue team to let Larson pass. Wasting no time, Larson disappears through the crevice.

INT. GORGE - NIGHT

That same night, Karen stands at the edge of a dried-up gorge, while TWO CHILDREN help her wrap the ranger's corpse into sheets.

After they're done, the bearded man helps Karen lift up the corpse to toss it down into the gorge.

BEARDED MAN
I radioed the League. They're on their way.

KAREN
Thank you. What is your name?

Their conversation continues as he and the children escort Karen back towards the ancient city ruins.

BEARDED MAN
I'm Enoch.

KAREN
(shaking his hand)
And I'm Captain Samuels. Is your nose going to be okay?

ENOCH
It's fine. Nothing to worry about. I'm truly sorry about the rangers.

KAREN

I'm sorry, too.

ENOCH

I hope you understand my position. My duty is to protect my people first and foremost.

KAREN

Why didn't you believe me before, when I told you about the League?

ENOCH

I had to assume you were a spy. I found out you were telling the truth when I saw your birthmark, but by then it was too late.

KAREN

So why didn't the draco attack me?

ENOCH

What happened today was an omen. It's what the people of Agartha have been waiting for.

KAREN

Agartha? Is that the name of your city?

ENOCH

Yes, my people, the Vril-ya, built it thousands of years ago. We've been enslaved since it was destroyed by the reptilian armies, but now, freedom has finally come.

KAREN

How do you know the draco won't be back?

ENOCH

He might. But his reign of terror is over. You see, the Black
Sun belongs to the Vril-ya and to all humans. It was a gift from
the Council of Elders of Orion. The draco stole it from us, but
now that you've arrived, we're going to get it back.

KAREN

I hope your people don't think I'm some kind of savior, Enoch.
I don't want to give them false hopes.

ENOCH

There's a lot you still don't know, Captain. The League will
train you to prepare for this battle. They will teach you to
summon your powers and master them.

KAREN

But I don't want to let you guys down. I could never fight like
you and Lita do. You guys are way too powerful.

ENOCH

Did you know that there was a time when all humans had
extraordinary powers? Lita and I only use a small fraction of the
power we all have potentially.

KAREN

(remembering)

Lita mentioned something about that, too. So you're saying we can all be like you guys?

ENOCH

That and even stronger, faster, much more powerful. The Sub Galactic League's mission is to recover the Black Sun so that humanity can get its powers back. It's the only way we can defeat the great white draco and his army of reptilians.

KAREN

But, if you're so concerned about the wellbeing of humans, why do you feed them to the draco?

ENOCH

Captain, the draco has been coming here every night since he stole our crystal, looking for people to eat. The enzymes in our brains are highly nutritious to him. He absorbs our power.

KAREN

What happens if you don't feed him?

ENOCH

He eats our own.

KAREN

I still don't understand what makes you think it's over.

ENOCH

Why do you think he spared your life?

KAREN

I'm not sure.

ENOCH

He saw something in you.

KAREN

Enoch, I—

ENOCH

How do you explain that birthmark?

KAREN

You think that's what made him leave?

ENOCH

You know that better than I do. Why are you so driven to find the Black Sun?

KAREN

I'm not quite sure. Maybe because I want to know the truth.

ENOCH

Or perhaps it's because you're destined for it and you can't avoid it, no matter how hard you try.

KAREN

I don't believe in fate, Enoch, I believe in free will.

ENOCH

And who's to say there is no free will within fate?

Karen stops to consider his words.

ENOCH (CONT'D)
(pointing ahead)
Oh, look! They're here.

As they return to Agartha, Karen sees that Enoch was referring to THE LEAGUE'S SAUCER, which has just landed outside the ruins.

The moment the kids see Caesar climb out of the saucer, they race towards him, SCREAMING in excitement.

ENOCH (CONT'D)
Well ... I guess this is goodbye. For now.

Karen shakes Enoch's hand.

KAREN

See you soon, Enoch. Thanks for being honest with me.

He smiles at her and waves goodbye.

CUT TO:

INT. VERTICAL SHAFT - DAY

Chief Larson has just climbed down the long ladder that leads to the bottom of the shaft. We recognize this as the same shaft where Lita's saucer first captured Karen.

As soon as he climbs down from the ladder, Larson shines a flashlight on the ground and finds A BURNT OUT FLARE. It is the flare we saw Karen drop all the way down from the top of the ladder.

He picks up the flare and examines it. He is about to dial a number on his cell phone, when he suddenly hears a noise behind him. Quickly, he spins around to see what it is and spots A SHADOWY MASS moving towards him in a tunnel.

CHIEF LARSON
Who's there?

As he shines his flashlight into the tunnel, we see A GROUP OF REPTILIANS emerging from the darkness.

They're the same type of reptilian creatures Karen encountered in the tunnels earlier, only these are a lot more coordinated and human-like in the way they move. They are wearing what appear to be BLACK MILITARY UNIFORMS.

CUT TO:

INT. SAUCER - DAY

Marcus conducts the saucer through miles and miles of CAV-
ERNOUS PITS, while Caesar and Lita talk to Karen.

CAESAR
Twenty-four hours?

KAREN
That's what he said.

LITA
But that's tonight!

CAESAR
He's going to come after us with everything he's got.

Lita and Caesar exchange concerned looks.

LITA
We're going to have to go with plan B.

CAESAR
(firmly)
No.

LITA
It's the only way, Caesar.

CAESAR
There's not enough time.

Karen's eyes dart back and forth between Caesar and Lita.

KAREN
What's plan B?

LITA
It's our only hope.

CAESAR
It's not safe.

KAREN
What are you guys talking about?

LITA
Marcus, take us to the dungeons.

CAESAR
Lita, I said no.

Ignoring Caesar's remark, Lita opens A COMPARTMENT and takes out A PORTABLE SCANNER with AN LCD-SCREEN and A PROBE attached to it.

LITA
Captain, you want to know the truth, don't you?

KAREN
Of course. That's why I'm here.

CAESAR
It's too dangerous, Captain. You don't have to agree.

KAREN
(to Caesar)
Then why did you bring me here?

LITA
We have to leave it up to her, Caesar. It's her call.

CAESAR
It's too much for her to handle all at once.

KAREN
It'd be easier if you told me what this is about.

CAESAR
(to Karen)
Are you willing to die if the plan fails?

KAREN

Listen to me, Libertador. I don't know what this very dangerous plan is, but what I do know is that the Vril-ya people are suffering. And, judging by what I've seen lately, I'm pretty sure the Colombians are, too. We're sitting here arguing while time is running out, and all you can do is ask me if I'm willing to die?

Caesar and Lita look at each other.

KAREN (CONT'D)

I think my presence here makes my answer to that question pretty obvious, don't you think?

Lowering his head, Caesar thinks for a moment, then sighs with resignation.

CAESAR

Okay then.
(turning to Marcus)
Marcus, to the dungeons please.

CUT TO:

INT. LAB - REPTILIAN BASE - DAY

Larson lies naked on an examination table, SCREAMING his heart out. His wrists and ankles are restrained with METAL

BRACES. There is a bright SURGICAL LAMP shining on his face. He's cut and bruised, and there are NUMEROUS CABLES hooked up to his head and chest. He squirms, trying to break free from the restraints but it's useless.

A REPTILIAN NURSE injects him with A SYRINGE, and he passes out almost instantly.

                                                      CUT TO:

INT. DUNGEONS - DAY

Lita leads Karen into AN ANCIENT DUNGEON rife with cob-webs and mold.

Karen covers her nose as the stench of ROTTEN FLESH creeps up her nostrils. Staring at her surroundings in disbelief, she slows down to look at the HUMAN SKELETONS hanging from the walls.

                          KAREN
          What is this? Some kind of torture chamber?

                           LITA
      It's the subterranean facility you've been looking for. We're in
                  the bottom level, which reminds me—

She takes out A METALLIC BRACELET and fastens it around

Karen's wrist.

Deeply intrigued, Karen stops to examine it.

KAREN
What's this for?

LITA
It's a magnetic bracelet. It throws off their surveillance systems.

They keep moving.

KAREN
So this is it, huh? The building on the blueprints?

LITA
Yup, we're about two miles underground, directly below the temple.

KAREN
Who are all these people that died here?

LITA
Abductees.

KAREN
Oh, come on, Lita. You don't mean abductees as in *alien* abductions, do you?

A bit irritated by Karen's skeptical tone, Lita turns around to face her.

LITA
You said you wanted the truth, right?

Karen nods sheepishly.

A little upset, Lita pulls out A BOOK OF MATCHES to light up a joint.

She takes a long, deep hit from it, and appears relieved once it kicks in.

LITA
You want a hit?

KAREN
No, thanks.

LITA
It'll calm your nerves.

KAREN
I'm calm. Just tell me what you're talking about.

LITA
The truth could be hard to handle.

KAREN

You mean to say those reptilian creatures are extraterrestrial?

Taking another hit from the joint, Lita presses forward, looking really frustrated.

LITA

You just got to have that empirical evidence staring you in the face, don't you?

KAREN

Oh, please, Lita. Admit it. It's just a little too farfetched, I mean—

LITA

Look. Bottom line is, if you really want the truth, you're going to have to forget all about the bullshit the military has fed you, alright?

KAREN

I'm not going to join the guerrillas if that's what you're driving at.

LITA

You really think this is about politics?

KAREN

Why are you guys working with the guerrillas then?

LITA

If it weren't for them, Caesar would be dead. They took him in
and taught him the strategies of guerrilla warfare.
(checking her watch)
But if you're having second thoughts, we can still turn around
and go back right now. We'll take you back up to the surface.

KAREN

No. I want to see whatever it is you want to show me.

INT. SAUCER - DAY

Caesar sits in front of the ASE, keeping watch on the base under
the temple. He keeps track of the girls' location in the building
by scanning their HEAT SIGNATURES with AN INFRARED
THERMOMETER.

Marcus glances over at Caesar and notices his intense concentration.

MARCUS

You shouldn't have let 'em go alone, man.

CAESAR

Shut up, Marcus.

MARCUS

She's still one of them, you know.

CAESAR
You're breaking my concentration.

MARCUS
She could be setting us up.

CAESAR
She isn't.

MARCUS
How can you be so sure?

CAESAR
Because I trust her. And Lita does, too.

MARCUS
Oh, for crying out loud, Caesar, who do you think you're kidding?

While they're busy arguing, the ASE senses Caesar's altered emotional state which, in turn, causes static interference.

CAESAR
We need her on our side.

MARCUS
You're way too naive, man. I bet the only reason she got close to us is because she wants to gather intel for her people.

CAESAR

She's this close to joining our cause. This close, you just watch.

MARCUS

She's gonna serve your ass on a platter to her daddy. That's what she's gonna do if you don't watch your back, man.

CAESAR

Look, Marcus, just let me and Lita handle this, alright? We know what we're doing.

MARCUS

Hey! I've been a member of the League way longer than you, pal. Don't you dare talk down to me.

CAESAR

No one's talking down to you. Stop tripping, man!

MARCUS

You wouldn't be half the man you are today if I hadn't introduced you to the League.

CAESAR

Maybe, but I proved myself worthy, so I earned my place.

MARCUS

What the fuck is your problem, man? You act like you're some kind of god. Always talking like you're better than everybody.

CAESAR

I just don't understand why you're trying to turn this into a competition. There's no rivalry between us, Marcus. You're the only one who feels inferior. We're both valuable in the eyes of the council. End of story.

MARCUS

Bullshit. You're a cocky, arrogant son of a bitch, that's what you are.

CAESAR

Whatever, man. Take a chill pill or something. I'm busy here.

MARCUS

I swear to god, Caesar, if that chick betrays us, I'll personally bring her down. I won't hesitate for a second. I will bring her down, man. You got that?

Even though the image on the ASE gets scrambled and loses its clarity every time Caesar's heart rate goes up, we can still distinguish THREE BODIES approaching the dungeons and coming dangerously close to where Lita and Karen are.

INT. CHAMBER - DAY

Meanwhile, Lita and Karen have entered a MORGUE-LIKE CHAMBER lit by GREEN FLUORESCENT LAMPS. SEVERAL HUMAN BODIES lie naked on examination tables.

They all appear to be in a VEGETATIVE STATE and are hooked up with tubes to LARGE BAGS OF FLUID.

KAREN

What the hell is this place?

LITA

This is where they bring the abductees. All their, quote and quote, *research* is done down in this lab.

KAREN

What kind of research?

LITA

The illegal kind. Scientific experimentation with human subjects, cloning, DNA modification, genetic fusion, you name it. It all goes down right here.

As Karen explores the chamber, her eyes flicker in the direction of a counter against the wall, on top of which she spots NUMEROUS VATS filled with AMNIOTIC FLUID.

Floating in the vats she discovers FETUSES of WINGED WHITE DRACOS. They're miniature versions of the draco that killed Sergeant Jimenez in Agartha.

Karen gets a little closer to examine them and is horrified when she sees that the UMBILICAL CORDS are all attached to

PLASTIC TUBES that hang above each vat. The tubes are, in turn, connected to the human bodies on the examination tables.

KAREN
So all these people are abductees?

LITA
They're not people anymore. Just "nutrients."

KAREN
Are they brain dead?

LITA
Yes, completely stripped of their identity. All their memories have been wiped out so their survival instinct is only strong enough to keep their hearts pumping.

Karen studies each of the vats until one of the fetuses suddenly OPENS ITS EYES. Startled out of her wits, Karen flinches backwards.

LITA
(chuckling)
They're harmless.

KAREN
(not fully convinced)
What are they?

LITA

Clones.

KAREN

But I thought there was only one winged white draco.

LITA

He's cloning himself.

KAREN

(shocked)

But we can't let that happen. We've got to stop him.

LITA

We will, but there's something we gotta do first.

Lita disconnects one of the human vegetables from the feeding tubes. The moment she does this, the VITAL SIGNS on the MONITOR next to him FLATLINE, followed by A CONSTANT ALERT BEEP.

KAREN

Stop! You're killing him!

Lita shuts off the monitor and the beeping stops.

LITA

Relax, Captain. He's as good as dead anyway. No conscious

awareness, no memories. I'm just setting him free so he can rest in peace.

Karen takes a step back and watches in utter disbelief as Lita uses the device she brought from the saucer to scan the corpse's brain.

Running the probe across the corpse's forehead, Lita searches for something in the area between the eyebrows. As A BARELY VISIBLE MASS flashes on the screen, Lita turns off the apparatus.

LITA (CONT'D)
Found it.

KAREN
What is it?

LITA
Hang on. You'll see.

Lita opens several drawers and closet doors until she finds A SLEDGE HAMMER. Karen cringes in disgust as Lita uses the sledge hammer to CRACK OPEN THE SKULL of the corpse.

KAREN
What are you doing?

Having put on latex gloves, Lita locates the PINEAL GLAND
AREA in the center of the now-exposed brain of the corpse.
After that, she uses a PAIR OF TWEEZERS to extract from it
the object the scanner detected: AN ELECTRONIC MICRO-
CHIP the size of a pea.

Karen's jaw drops open, and, once again, her nose starts bleeding.

LITA

Here.

(hands her a tissue)

Do you ever wonder why your nose bleeds every time you get

déjà vu?

The realization hits Karen like a thunderbolt.

KAREN

Déjà vu? Are you saying I've got one of those implants, too?

LITA

(nods)

Duh! And that, my friend, is what's keeping you from remem-

bering your past.

INT. SAUCER - DAY

Back in the saucer, Caesar has just spotted the THREE BODIES on the ASE. He sees that they're about to walk in on Karen and Lita, so he immediately flips on the com-link.

CAESAR
Lita, do you read me?

LITA (O.S.)
Come in, Caesar. What's going on?

CAESAR
You got reptilians heading your way. Get out now!

INT. CHAMBER - DAY

Karen can tell by the look on Lita's face that something's terribly wrong, but, before she even has time to ask, she suddenly hears FOOTSTEPS approaching the door.

Pulling out her FLASH GUN, Lita drops the sledge hammer on the floor and takes shelter in the shadows under one of the examination tables. Karen dives under a nearby counter just as the door opens.

KAREN'S POV: TWO REPTILIAN HUMANOIDS wearing white lab coats enter the chamber. They drag A MAN toward the area where the human vegetables lie in their near-death sleep. It is dark, so Karen can barely make out their shapes as they enter. The man is wearing a hospital gown, and his head hangs low like he is drifting in and out of consciousness.

Karen recognizes the reptilians to be the same kind of three-toed bipedal creatures she encountered in the tunnels, only now she's able to see them more clearly under the dim light.

An alien species different from the winged white dracos, the reptilians are genetically-engineered hybrids. They are half-human/ half-reptile just like Jimenez said. They have grayish-green scaly skin and stand at about 8 ft. from the ground. No wings or tail, with claw-like webbed fingers and huge, slanted, glowing-red eyes with vertical slit pupils.

As one of the reptilians lays the man down flat on AN EXAMI-NATION TABLE, the other reptilian turns on the SURGICAL LAMP above the table. Karen almost passes out from shock as she sees the MAN'S FACE under the pool of bright white light.

CLOSE ON: The man's face. It is CHIEF LARSON. His droopy eyelids and zombielike expression make it obvious that he's been drugged. Even though he doesn't resist what the reptilians are doing, his eyes reflect a PROFOUND, HELPLESS DREAD.

KAREN
(whispering to herself)
Chief!

Right as one of the reptilians is about to insert AN IMPLANT into Larson's brain through his nostril, Karen crawls over to the sledge hammer and picks it up.

The two reptilian scientists stand there, slack-jawed, as Karen comes out of the shadows, swinging the sledge hammer at them.

KAREN (CONT'D)
(screaming)
Chief, run!

But Larson is too sedated to register what is going on. Meanwhile, Lita is so thrown off by Karen's reaction, that she, too, blows her own cover and busts out of her hideout.

LITA
Captain, stop!

Ignoring Lita, Karen DECAPITATES one of the reptilians with a single swing of the sledge hammer. Then, as she is about to attack the other one, the creature SHRIEKS LOUDLY and makes a dash for the door.

Lita shoots at it with the flash gun several times, and the reptilian drops to the floor, bleeding.

In the mean time, Karen grabs the chief and helps him off the examination table.

LARSON
Captain, is that you?

KAREN
Yes, sir! What the hell are you doing here?

LARSON
I came looking for you.

Karen hugs the chief tightly.

KAREN
Oh, Chief, you shouldn't have done that.

LITA
(clearing her throat)
Don't mean to break up the party, but we need to get out of here fast, Captain.

KAREN
Help me carry him.

Larson struggles to keep his balance, but his legs are too weak and he keeps falling over.

LITA
Excuse me? There's no way Caesar and Marcus are going to let us back on the vessel with this guy!

KAREN
He's in this mess because of me, so he's coming with us.

LITA
I'm sorry, Captain, but, as far as the League's concerned, he's
the enemy.

KAREN
The enemy? Are you listening to yourself? You saw what they
were about to do to him.

Lita and Karen are so focused on their argument, that they don't
notice the reptilian scientist Lita shot down has regained consciousness. As Karen and Lita continue arguing over Larson,
the reptilian slowly drags itself towards the entrance through
which it came, leaving a trail of fresh blood behind it.

LITA
You can't trust him anymore, Captain. You gotta come with us.

CHIEF LARSON
Captain, go with her. I'll be alright.

But Karen can plainly see that Larson is much too weak to even
walk on his own.

KAREN
I'm staying right here with you, Chief.

Just then, the reptilian scientist reaches the entrance and is able to stretch out its arm just high enough to reach A CONTROL PANEL by the doorway. Right before he drops dead, the reptilian presses a button on the panel and TRIPS AN ALARM.

By the time Lita and Karen realize the creature used up its last reserve of life to warn the others, A PIERCING, HIGH-PITCHED SOUND BLASTS throughout the chamber.

LITA
(growing desperate)
I understand your predicament, Captain, I really do, but we can all kiss our asses goodbye if we stay here any longer.

KAREN
You said you wanted to help me. Well, this is your chance to show me you meant it.

Lita looks around and considers her options.

There are no outlets in sight except for the main entrance, which is now a mess of flashing, red-alert lights.

LITA
It's not that simple. We can't jeopardize our mission. You have to make a choice now. There's no middle ground. You either stay with him or you come with us.

CAESAR (O.S.)
(via com-link, through interference)
Lita, I'm losing you. What the hell is going on down there?

LITA
(into com-link)
Caesar, I need an emergency exit right now. Do you read me?

CAESAR (O.S.)
That lab is going to be swarming with reptilian soldiers in less
than a minute. What the hell are you guys waiting for?

While Lita and Caesar talk on the com-link, Karen examines the
tubes that connect the vats to the human vegetables. She follows
their course with her eyes and notices they all converge at the
same corner of a wall and are all bundled up and strapped to the
floor with a plastic fastener.

Karen rushes toward the corner and notices that the bundle of
tubes snakes through A SMALL REMOVABLE GRATE on the
floor.

Wasting no time, she removes the grate and takes a peek down
through the opening. Next to the bundled tubes, she sees a
narrow opening with scarcely room enough for a single person
to pass through.

She quickly looks through the opening and discovers A VERTI-

CAL PASSAGEWAY with a METAL LADDER that leads down to AN ENGINE ROOM.

Her mind made up, Karen shoots across the room and finds her way back to the chief. She then drags him along with her until they reach the opening on the floor.

KAREN
Lita! This way!

Lita doesn't move.

LITA
You go on, Captain.

As Karen helps a very drowsy Larson climb down the metal ladder, she hesitates before following after him.

KAREN
Lita, come with us, please!

Lita waits until Karen is halfway down the ladder and then grabs the grate.

LITA
Someone has to stay behind to hold them back.

Karen reluctantly reaches the last rung of the ladder.

KAREN

There's too many of them for you to take on alone. The League has to understand that, please Lita.

LITA
(unwilling to budge)
So long, Captain.

Karen finds herself surrounded by darkness as Lita covers the opening with the grate.

INT. ENGINE ROOM - CONTINUOUS

By the time Karen drops down into the room below, Larson has blindly felt his way through the darkness and down the CON-CRETE WALLS. Having found the light switch, he flips it up, and the room becomes flooded with sudden brightness.

KAREN
You okay there, Chief?

CHIEF LARSON
Yeah.
(coughs)
I'll live.

Karen examines her surroundings and continues to follow the path of the bundled tubes with her eyes. She sees that they all end up connected to a row of TALL INDUSTRIAL CISTERNS lined up against the walls.

KAREN

I'm really going to need you to wake up because I think I may have just found us a way out of here.

CHIEF LARSON

(looking around, confused)

Where?

KAREN

Through there.

She points at the water in the cisterns, and the chief observes how it gets funneled and emptied out into AN UNDER-GROUND RESERVOIR at the far end of the engine room.

CHIEF LARSON

That water must be freezing.

Just then, LOUD NOISES are heard from the chamber above. Karen hears Lita's flash gun SHOOTING and the now-familiar SHRIEKS from the reptilians as they get hit. She looks up at the ladder, then back at the chief and hesitates.

The noises grow louder with furniture SLAMMING on the floor, GLASS SHATTERING and more STRIDENT SCREAMS.

KAREN
We have to help her.

CHIEF LARSON
You did everything you could, Captain. She made her choice
just like you made yours. Now we need to keep moving or her
sacrifice will be in vain.

Larson is barely finished saying this, when A LOUD BOOM
GOES OFF, and the room upstairs suddenly EXPLODES INTO
A BALL OF FLAMES, blasting through the grate above the
ladder and causing the structure to crumble down into large
chunks of concrete and twisted metal.

Even though the flames don't reach Karen and the chief, the
impact of the explosion still sends them both flying through the
air and straight into the:

INT. RESERVOIR TANK - CONTINUOUS

The moment their bodies hit the water, Karen and the chief
SCREAM OUT as the FREEZING COLD engulfs them suddenly.

CHIEF LARSON
Captain, hold on to me!

The reservoir mechanism seems to be wired with MOTION

SENSORS, which get activated automatically, because, as soon as they make contact with the water, AN ALARM GOES OFF. Only seconds later, A ROUND METAL LID slides open at the bottom of the reservoir tank, immediately sucking Karen and the chief into an:

INT. INDUSTRIAL DRAINING PIPE - CONTINUOUS

Karen and Larson get violently propelled down the pipe, carried by the raging water that is also being forced down from the tank.

TO BE CONTINUED...

www.ingramcontent.com/pod-product-compliance
Lightning Source LLC
Chambersburg PA
CBHW051454170626
46811CB00002B/478